KNIC

THE SUN

J P Walker

Beaten Track

www.beatentrackpublishing.com

Knights of the Sun

First published 2013 by Beaten Track Publishing
Copyright © 2013 J P Walker

A CIP catalogue record for this book
is available from the British Library.

ISBN: 978 1 909192 44 7

Beaten Track Publishing,
Burscough. Lancashire.
www.beatentrackpublishing.com

For Myah

Chapter One

Smoke.

It was everywhere.

Watching movies as a boy, Dr. Pete Standon's preconceived notion of fire was blazing flames and freakish heat, but this was definitely the worst part; all this smoke. Raphael's hospital, where Pete worked, had been engulfed in this infernal smoke for hours, though to him it felt a lot longer. No one had yet been able to inform him of the cause of the fire; no doubt once everyone was safe and this cursed event had been investigated they would be told it was due to the hospital's poor electrical system or some other entirely avoidable factor. For now, Pete continued with his efforts to rescue patients from the second floor—those sent from the E.R., suffering non-fatal injuries but still needing observation.

He was on that floor now, helping an elderly gentleman sporting a bandage on his right ankle. The man was not Pete's patient, so he did not know his name; he could only offer support in an impersonal way, and it felt wrong to him. In his mind, however, he had already nicknamed the man 'Mr. Limps', as a way to push himself to carry this man out of the fire. Mr. Limps was a little overweight, a couple of buttons of his blue striped pyjamas had come undone around the belly area, exposing a patch of hairy flab, his hair was very thin on top, his ankle straining with the weight upon it.

As the two struggled down the corridor on the second floor, Pete could barely see more than a few inches in front of him. Only when he felt others bumping into him as they ran, or he heard them screaming as they scrambled past, did he know that there were other survivors in the hospital, and once he had this information, he vowed to himself that every one of these patients would be joining the others in the fresh air. The shrill of the fire alarm really wasn't helping matters, for it was near impossible to keep shouting encouragement over it and breathe at the same time. The noise coming from the fire alarm was just that: noise, and it was quickly becoming unbearably painful, with a loud, hiss-like quality that was hurting Pete's ears, to the point where he wondered if they might actually be bleeding.

"I'm sure it didn't sound like this when the fire started. Must've been listening to it for too long," he thought to himself, hoping it would distract and keep him calm, although his panic was slowly subsiding as he and Mr. Limps made their way to the fire escape—Pete knew they were almost at the door because he could see the black smoke being sucked through the small open space as if it too were trying to flee. They stepped outside and were at once greeted by glorious sunshine and flawless blue sky. Pete took in deep breaths as a paramedic rushed up the spiral metal staircase towards them and helped Mr. Limps down. The man turned in Pete's direction and for the first time he could see his eyes; they were a deep brown colour and he found himself wishing he had gotten to know him, for his eyes possessed intuition and wisdom. The man bestowed Pete with a gentle smile of thanks, unable to verbalise his gratitude.

The paramedic helped the older man to ground level and returned to assist Pete down the spiral staircase, which clinked and clanged as they made their way down, until he was finally able to observe the scene below him. There were three bright red, shiny fire engines placed around the hospital, at least eight ambulances and at least five police cars. All of the vehicles had their lights flashing, which, after having only black smoke for company, were as bright as fireworks. But the things that struck him most—and made him almost as sad as he was scared—were all the people; hundreds of them. Patients, doctors, nurses, paramedics, police, fire fighters; all running in different directions, sometimes colliding with each other, shouting rushed apologies as they continued urgently on their way. Raphael's hospital of Seattle, was no longer the harmonious environment that Pete had looked forward to working in every morning, it was pandemonium; chaotic and frightening. He knew from surveying this scene that his beloved city would never be the same. Never again would it feel like the blanket of safety that he had grown to appreciate.

On a grassy area next to the hospital's far too small car park and surrounded by tall trees, patients and staff unable to walk were sitting or lying. Many of them had their faces in their hands, some were crying, some were shouting but the majority of them were just holding onto one another. As Pete watched them comforting each other, he too felt a need to connect with someone and draw comfort from an embrace.

But then the moment passed as the shrill of the fire alarm brought him out of his contemplations and remembered the people still trapped inside. Running down the stairs, he grabbed the arm of the first official he could see—a bulky police officer, still wearing his sunglasses, shouting and gesturing for people to move aside.

"There are still people inside!" Pete said, pointing up at the building. The policeman briefly glanced at Pete, and then back up towards the chaos. He put a hand on his back to push him on.

"Sir, please keep moving! We're doing all we can."

"But they'll die! They can't see where they're going! Please go help them!" Pete was desperate. He knew this man could do nothing himself, but surely he could ensure the right people would go and get them? The policeman looked irritated, and grabbed Pete by the arm, their faces only inches apart; even with his sunglasses, Pete could tell he was being looked straight in the eye. The voice was calm, clear and almost threatening.

"There are plenty of people out here that need help. We are doing our best. Move to one side or help the injured. Either way, stop bothering me. I'm busy."

He released Pete's arm and continued gesturing people to move away from the fire escape, shouting instructions to other members of the rescue team. Pete glared at the police officer once more, then surveyed the scene around him. Everyone was running to help, trying to serve, to protect and rescue and here he was, being told to 'move aside'. With that, Pete Standon made his decision. He turned back towards the clanging spiral staircase and the fire escape. The police officer grabbed his arm in an attempt to stop him, but Pete just yanked it free and ran up the stairs two at a time.

As he stepped through the fire escape, he was met by more smoke. There seemed to be so much more of it now that his white shirt was grey and his tanned hands were black. He squinted as he tried to home in on the desperate voices.

"Hello? If you can hear me, walk towards me! I'm a doctor..." His calls were interrupted as he broke down coughing and gasping for air. He put his hands over his mouth but to no avail; he was struggling for breath. Still he persisted forward, even though he could not see in front of him, the thick black clouds swirling around and filling the hallway. He was losing his balance; walking was becoming so difficult, his feet dragging like dead weights along the floor. He reached out with his right hand, his left covering his mouth and nose, but he could find nothing against which to steady himself—no wall or chair, just smoke, and as he strained to keep moving, his legs gave out. Pete crumpled to the floor. The shrill squeal of the fire alarm seemed impossibly loud now, his ears aching with the noise and he couldn't breathe. Why were his eyes closing? He didn't want them to, he needed to get up. He tried in vain to lift himself using his elbows but they collapsed and he was flat on the floor, no sound of people running past, just him and the infernal scream of that fire alarm.

Then, very gently, almost in slow motion, a hand touched his; the softest fingers brushed across his fingers, gripped his hand and began pulling him up. His legs were suddenly strong again; they had stopped shaking. He took in a long deep breath and didn't taste smoke. He could breathe normally, although he still couldn't see. Squinting through the smoke, he could make out only a white blurry figure, with what looked like long dark hair but he couldn't name the colour. From the softness and size of the hand he suspected it was a woman. The most surprising and comforting thing of all was that he could no longer hear the fire alarm—had it been turned off? He heard nothing but a calm silence that filled the hallway, and as his rescuer gently led him forward, the smoke dispersed at her feet, slowly rising left and right as if clearing a path for her.

"Is everyone else OK?" Pete asked, fighting the urge to scream. He feared that the fire alarm may still be going off and he had gone completely deaf, desperately hoping that this was not the case. And what was that he could smell? The faintest hint of lavender—was it the smoke?

"They're fine, Pete, just follow me." The figure didn't turn her head—she was speaking barely above a whisper, but Pete heard her and continued to allow her to lead him towards the fire escape.

"You know me? Are you a doctor or nurse? What's your name?" These were strange things to be asking, he knew, but the questions were falling out of his mouth; he needed to know who she was. They were nearing the fire escape; he could see the smoke being sucked out again and sunshine getting closer.

"My name is Veil. Watch your step." As she spoke these words, Pete was outside, shielding his eyes from the too bright sun with his hand—the hand that Veil had been holding, but now she was gone. He looked down the staircase as paramedics raced up to greet him; the fire alarm screech had returned and he was feeling weak again. He allowed the paramedics to guide him down the stairs towards the ambulances and this time he didn't fight them, for he knew he needed oxygen, but he continued to scan the area in search of Veil. He couldn't find her.

He was being led by a paramedic with long hair in a ponytail—a man with strong arms and hands, gently guiding him past the roar of people and vehicles to the furthest ambulance, where he was sat down and an oxygen mask placed over his face. The paramedic examined him with concerned grey eyes and a soft smile. Pete took some deep, grateful breaths, his eyes once again roaming the area in search of Veil. When he looked back, the paramedic was gone. Pete pulled the mask from his face and stumbled out of the ambulance, frantically scanning the area, now searching for both Veil and the paramedic. There were so many people and it was hard to distinguish any facial features; everyone was beginning to look the same. He looked across the street, to where there were no people or flashing lights, and saw a small group of figures slowly walk away and turn down an alley. He recognised Veil immediately, her dark purple hair blowing in the wind and he could just about make out her profile. The other figures were doctors, nurses, fire fighters and the paramedic who had helped him in the ambulance. Pete ran across the street to chase after them. He was beginning to have difficulty breathing, but pushed on, running faster and faster, until he reached the alley.

He saw no one. Just bricks and windows and trash cans. But he could smell something. He closed his eyes and concentrated on that smell, smiling as a wave of tranquillity washed over him. The smell was lavender.

"Veil," he thought to himself. "What a great name."

***

They stood in their hundreds, a million miles from Earth, looking down at the hospital; people were still hurt and the building was going to need a vast amount of work in order to have it back to the way it was before, but the chaos had dissipated and no one was trapped. Shye took a step forward and smiled, a broad, heartfelt smile that lit up his blue-grey eyes. He reached behind him and pulled the tie from his hair freeing it from the ponytail—thick, wavy, chestnut hair that framed his face and cascaded over his broad shoulders. He glanced up in front of him and saw Dusk looking his way and smiling; he smiled back and noticed she too had returned her incredibly long blonde hair to its natural state, flowing to her hips and free to move in the breeze; Shye loved it most when it was like this; he loved to watch it being blown around. As he drank in all of her beautiful face, he lingered on her eyes: the clearest green, resembling a glass wine bottle when the sun shines through it. There was such vibrancy and happiness in those eyes, but also an element of regret and withdrawal. Shye recognised those emotions, for his eyes were filled with them every day.

Reluctantly he drew away from Dusk and looked to the rest of his team, feeling an astounding pride for what they had achieved. Many people in the hospital were saved today; the fire hadn't been anticipated—certainly not the amount of smoke that managed to weave its way throughout the entire building. He and his fellow Guardians had rescued more than they thought possible and in time would return to help rebuild the hospital, but for now the rescue teams had it under control. Shye took in everyone who had landed back home; there were thirty altogether: a big group for a big cause. Everyone was pleased with what they had accomplished that day, and the first timers were talking excitedly about the roles they had played; various police officers, paramedics and doctors blending in on Earth if only for a few short hours. His gaze shifted from the crowd, to take in their home, Aureia. After all his years there, the beauty of it could still take his breath away; such a sense of peace.

Behind his team stood the homes of thousands of Guardians, modest houses built with their own hands and resembling large huts, bunk-bedded on top of one another, creating enough space for two families. There were no roads in Aureia; the small kingdom was placed between Earth and Heaven before Earth had a name, and there was one tall building—so tall, in fact, that no one could see the top of it, no matter how long they looked up at it. This tower was known as Unenda, miles away from the little houses, with no doors or windows and Guardians were forbidden from it. Shye was one of the few who knew the reason for this, because Sol had told him. Sol, the leader and creator of their world, was a Sun priestess, the last of her kind and for as long as she had ruled over Aureia, the city had seen neither sunset nor dark cloud. Sol created and kept it a place of eternal light; everything was touched by sunshine, no darkness and no shadows. That was Shye's favourite thing about Aureia; no shadows. He, like every other Guardian, was afraid of the dark, and forbidden to fly to Earth after sunset for this reason—not that Shye ever would. He loved being in Aureia and hated to leave, no matter how brief the trip to Earth was.

He turned his attention back to the Guardians that had returned to Aureia with him. They were all smiling and few had retracted their wings; he could feel his own wings, powerful against the breeze, moving gently against his back. Shye had one of the biggest pairs of wings, almost ten feet in span and very impressive, with 30,000 feathers, each tinted reddish brown, just like the colour of Shye's hair. Every feather had its purpose and each one helped him fly; if one feather of his wings was hurt in some way, every other feather felt the pain. At the hollow of his throat was a pendant on an unbreakable silver chain, the pendant bore a remarkable resemblance to his own wings and appeared to have every feather in place, just like his real ones, and when the light hit it, there were hints of gold and brown.

As Shye continued to scan the group and his home, he realised someone was missing and he felt anger rise through him, for one Guardian on that day's mission had behaved recklessly. It was his unwanted duty to chastise the individual and he knew their whereabouts. In the middle of Aureia, with a large, wide space surrounding it, was a gap in the clouds above Earth. Five miles in diameter, it allowed the Guardians to look down to Earth, to see those they were guarding and monitor progress on a mission. This was the Window and it allowed Guardians to see anyone, anywhere on Earth.

Shye gently closed his eyes and with a grim smile on his face, he reached up and grasped the pendant to his chest, then pressed it to his heart. His wings began to glow with a bright orange light, then slowly disappeared as if receding into his back. When they were gone, he started walking towards the Window, knowing who he would find there.

Chapter Two

As Shye got closer, he could make out the figure of a girl lying on her stomach, her hands holding her head up, perched on her elbows, her feet waving gently in the air. Shye could see that her wings had already retracted and she looked like a little girl watching her favourite TV show, completely engrossed and loving every minute of it. Only a few metres away but still not being noticed, Shye cleared his throat loudly and laughed when the young woman in front of him jumped in surprise, although she did not move from her position.

"Shye! Don't sneak up on me. I don't like it," the girl said. She continued to gaze down through the Window, feigning annoyance.

Shye didn't speak. He looked at Veil, waiting for an apology, or at the very least an explanation for her thoughtless behaviour that day. Veil in turn was waiting for Shye to say something, anything regarding their mission at the hospital. She felt intimidated by his stance and intense stare and smiled up at him. It was not returned.

"I'm not looking at anyone in particular. I'm just checking on the hospital. We did good today."

Still Shye did not speak. His thick hair was blowing into his eyes but he made no attempt to remove it; his arms remained crossed over his chest. Eventually Veil gave up and retuned her gaze to the Window. They stayed quiet for a few moments more before Shye spoke, but didn't look at her.

"Do you have any idea what you risked today with that little stunt you pulled?" He clenched his jaw in an effort to stop himself from shouting. Veil blinked a few times, taken aback by his tone.

"By rescuing people from a burning building?" she countered. Before the last word was out of her mouth, Shye had moved quickly and yanked her to her feet with a firm grip on her bicep. They stood toe to toe and he was glaring down into her eyes, his own brimming with anger and judgement.

"You nearly exposed yourself—exposed all of us—for the sake of one human. ONE! It was irresponsible and dangerous and it's happened too many times recently. You are assigned to guard this human when it is called for, and today it was not. You had no need to enter that hospital and retrieve him, a fire fighter or paramedic would have found him. He would have been fine and you knew that." He released her arm and she stumbled backward, quickly regained her footing and raised her chin in defiance. Her eyes shone with confusion, pain, and also conviction. She looked as if she had been struck across the face, yet was ready to return a blow of her own. Tears burned in her eyes but she refused to let them fall.

"I am Pete Standon's Guardian. I have vowed to protect him, no matter the circumstance, danger or consequence. My personal feelings for him do not and will not ever cloud my judgement or ability to do just that. I was given no assurances that he would be safe today, so I took action, to shield him from the dangers in that hospital. And if fire fighters and police officers on Earth are so capable, why then do we have to do all the work for them?" She said her piece and glared angrily at Shye, awaited a response.

"Your personal feelings? Veil, you shouldn't have personal feelings towards him! You shouldn't be here at the Window, night after night watching him! One day you'll get yourself killed, putting his life and needs above your own and those of Aureia." Shye gestured as he said these words, pointing down through the Window.

"How dare you!" Veil shouted, trying to stare him down, "How dare you criticise my ability to guard Pete, to save his life, to keep him safe! What if it were Dusk in that building? Would you have left her?"

Shye looked shocked; admittedly, he had not thought of that. If it were Dusk in that situation, he knew that he would have done exactly the same thing. He looked down at his feet and shrugged like a young boy reprimanded for careless behaviour. Veil sighed and continued.

"Pete is the only half decent human down there." She looked down through the Window. On Earth, the sun was setting and night was the only time Guardians were not permitted to fly. "We are there as police, fire fighters, paramedics, teachers and whatever else they need us to be in order to get through each day. They are so weak without us, Shye, it's pathetic. Pete exudes a light and strength that leaves the rest of them in shadow and—I'm in love with him." As she spoke the last few words, her voice reduced to a whisper and fresh tears sprung to her eyes.

Shye's face softened greatly and sympathy filled his eyes; he struggled to find the right words to say. Even so, the reality of the situation needed to be addressed.

"You think he is strong, beautiful and glowing because you love him, Veil. When I looked at that man today in my ambulance, he was just a man, covered in soot and smelling of smoke. He looked tired, weak and mortal. You were chosen as his Guardian, to protect and guide when it is asked of you, no more can ever happen. Pete can not even know that you exist. I know how painful this is, believe me. You can force a broken heart back together, but there are always too many pieces left behind and inevitably there'll always be something missing and so your heart…never really beats as it should." Shye's voice had lost all of its harshness, now just soft and compassionate.

Veil regarded her large friend; he stood just over a foot taller than herself, and she was shocked that he understood exactly how she was feeling. She returned to her previous position and continued to watch Pete. He was walking towards a corner store, still covered in black smudges and looking exhausted. Shye watched also; even after his small tirade he too could see something special within Pete Standon. He laid down on his front next to Veil, resting his chin in his hand and slyly casting his eyes over his friend. He wished she wouldn't torment herself in this manner, for he understood the feeling all too well. Veil was incredibly beautiful; he took in her pale, flawless skin, her long silky hair with its purple tinge that matched her eyes perfectly—they were a dark purple colour but would lighten when she was happy, and as he breathed in her scent he smiled at that ever familiar lavender aroma that was just Veil. After being regarded for a long time, Veil turned and looked back at Shye before speaking.

"So, my dear friend, are you ever going to tell Dusk how you feel about her?"

Struck by the question, Shye didn't really know how to answer. He took his gaze away from Veil's and looked down into the Window again, searching for an answer that he would rather deliver than the truth; he finally decided that the truth would be the best option. He exhaled and dropped his hand from his chin, allowing it to swing freely by the clouds' edge.

"No, Veil, I'm not. There's too much risk involved. I would give my life before I let any harm come to her. As you know, if I were to voice my feelings for Dusk and if we were to be joined, it would only be a matter of time before I was responsible for her fall from Aureia."

"You wouldn't be responsible, Shye, but I know what could happen; you could join and live forever as one. If I had that option…" Veil couldn't finish her sentence. She fell quiet for a moment to collect herself, then grabbed Shye's hand, forcing eye contact once again before she spoke, with determination.

"Love is always worth the risk, Shye, whether it be for one day or a millennium. And your heart deserves every beat, with no parts missing." As she said this, her gaze fell back down to Pete, and she felt Shye nodding in agreement beside her. He had a lot to think about.

When she realised she could take no more of this torment, Veil slowly rose to her feet, her dark purple hair catching the breeze. Shye followed suit. As he stood to his full height, Veil had to look up to see his face. She cast one last glance down through the Window and then they began walking back to the group, unaware that everything was about to change.

**

A million miles away from Aureia was a parallel land of darkness and dread. Every inch of this world was shadow, rain and fog. For miles and miles the only visible elements were the moments when lightning would strike in a bright fierce line along the ground, making it shake with every bolt.

Stormcry.

It was laden with clouds at every edge, tinted with dark, angry reds and deep, impenetrable blues; it appeared a truly menacing and angry place. Large, angular rocks spread moderately, jutting through the clouds as if they were mountain peaks. The largest of these peaks was home to the ruler of this world; along its vertical edge was a crack wide enough to fit a thousand men; it stretched along the full length of the cliff, and straight down.

There was a figure looking through the crack, almost as if inspecting it; a cloaked man, bent on one knee, his forearm resting on it with his hand loosely dangling over. He was gently rubbing his fingers together, causing small blue sparks to appear between the pale bony appendages. A harsh, dark rain was thrashing against his side, his long, black, stringy hair blown across his face, and through it red pupils zeroed in on something, like a cat watching a mouse, eyes darting around, wild with excitement.

Through the crack, he saw a dismal and very typical street, with leaves beginning to fall from trees, a small corner store and a customer leaving the establishment, carrying a plastic bag that hung loosely and occasionally bumped against his leg.

***

Pete Standon left the store with his six pack of beer, the tiny bell above the door jingling as he exited. He was in his neighbourhood: Northgate. Pete always found this place to be friendly, the kind of place where neighbours still said 'hello' and offer smiles whenever they pass each other. Exhausted from the events at the hospital that day, he walked slowly, his feet felt like they were filled with lead and he willed them to carry him to his apartment building;

it was only a ten minute walk from the store. He hadn't even gone home to shower yet, just wanting a drink—something he rarely needed to steady his nerves—and to walk among the streets to breathe clean air. His clothes were still covered with soot, he could still smell smoke on his shirt. His face was black and streaked, and his eyes were red, both from the fumes at the hospital and because he had been crying. He could still hear the yells of terror and pain as he helped the patients and other doctors out of the hospital.

He was also thinking about the mystery woman that had saved his life. *Veil*, he thought, wondering if he was ever going to see her again. He relived those moments with her, imagining her voice, the softness of her hand in his and the way her presence had made him feel so safe. Indeed, his thoughts were so consumed by his rescuer that he didn't notice the two large men begin to follow him down the street. He was further from shops and streetlights now; the street was darker and he slowly became aware of the footsteps behind him, growing louder and faster as they caught up with him. Without turning back to look, and even though he was exhausted, he quickened his pace, almost running; so too did his followers, and soon he could feel their presence close at his back.

He thought he might be safe, as there were a few other people on the streets, but just as he allowed this thought to give him some comfort, he was knocked to the ground by arms around his waist, as the smaller of the men wrestled him down and started to punch him in the ribs. Everything was happening so fast, Pete was powerless to stop it, feebly trying to push his attackers' hands away and put his own up in order to protect his face. To no avail though, as the second assailant began kicking aggressively at his legs, causing him to cry out as a particularly harsh blow hit his knee with a crunch.

***

High above in Stormcry, the figure continued watching through the crack at this unfolding attack, his red pupils shifting from the event happening beneath him to a girl standing at his side. She had crimson hair that made her already pale face look even whiter, the stinging rain, hitting her in the face and partly obscuring her vision, drips falling from the pointed tips of her hair and running down her face. Even in her current crouched position, the girl, although small, radiated a perilous poise, both beneficial and dangerous. Her eyes, the colour of tarnished silver, observed the scene below, watching the movements of the assailants with rapt attention and a gleam of appreciation. She was in position, ready to jump down to Earth, gripping the edges of the precipice and rocking on her heels. She turned to Vulgaar and those red eyes took her in again; he grinned—a wicked, twisted smile—and delivered a small nod. At this she shifted all of her weight on to the balls of her feet and fell forward over the edge of the crack, towards Earth.

***

Pete was screaming for help as his attackers overpowered him and beat him further into the pavement, but no one stopped to help. Onlookers and passersby quickly considered the situation and then fled the scene, leaving Pete helpless and hopeless. He could feel blood pouring from his nose and a heavy pounding in his head. His vision was beginning to blur…

He squinted at the pair of feet as they landed in front of his face, as if they had jumped from a ledge above. With the feet came a rain that began to gently beat against his face, a relief from the blows occupying his nose and cheeks, and with that relief darkness. The two large men, dishevelled and howling with amusement, continued their assault, even though their victim had lost consciousness. With the help of the new arrival, a young woman with crimson hair, they continued to strike Pete as he lay on the floor, no longer moving. Onlookers took the road of self-preservation, avoiding the violence and praying that someone would be brave enough to stop it.

Chapter Three

Veil had returned to the Window, unable to stay away, taking her favourite spot on her front and resting her delicate chin in her elegant hands. She watched and listened as Pete's tired voice requested a six pack in his local shop, relieved that he was almost home. She winced as he tried to walk, and knew his legs and feet were tired and aching as he trudged up the street. It was dark and late and she felt very uneasy watching him alone at this hour. The distant rolling of thunder clouds made her uneasy; frightened. She and every other Guardian hated the sound of thunder. She was so engrossed in watching her favourite person that she hadn't noticed Dusk and Shye come to her side, until Shye cleared his throat loudly and grinned shyly at her. She briefly returned the smile, noticing that he had pulled his wavy locks back into a tie behind his head. He looked downward, to Pete, as he walked out of the shop with his purchase; they all watched him quietly, until Dusk broke the silence.

"He looks in pain," she observed with sympathy in her eyes.

"He's had a rough day," Veil replied and a tear rolled down her face as she said it. She stood and faced her friends, a light breeze blowing some of her shiny purple hair into her face, which she gracefully swept away with her hand. She watched as Shye and Dusk exchanged uncomfortable glances. Shye gave her a reassuring smile and a nod. Dusk took a tentative step forward and touched Veil's shoulder before speaking.

"Veil, as you know, no human has ever met their Guardian. It is forbidden. Who knows what would come to pass for Pete or yourself, should he ever come to know who you are. I know your feelings for this man run deeper than you can bear; however, you are his Guardian and not his friend. You are entrusted with his safety and as such, must try and stay away from him, for his own good." When she had finished she looked to Shye, who smiled yet kept his air of authority. They both turned to Veil, who looked at them, shocked.

"What are you telling me, Dusk? That I can not care for Pete and guard his life at the same time? If I didn't care, I couldn't guard, simple as that. I am his Guardian and I care about him and his safety." She looked straight into Dusk's eyes and lowered her voice to a growl. "Don't ever question that again."

As she made this last statement she looked back down to Pete walking along the street, his six pack securely in his hands. She heard the footsteps closing in on him so clearly that she could have been walking beside him. Shye took a step forward, a challenge in his eyes as he moved in front of Dusk and towered over Veil.

"Don't threaten her, Veil. We're only trying to help. My approach earlier didn't appear to have comforted you any. I asked Dusk for her assistance." He glanced down through the Window—that large gap in the clouds which he secretly wished he could cover up every now and then. "No good will come of watching him incessantly. Come away from here, before you break down completely."

Veil had stopped listening. She felt a dread wash over her soul; her heartbeat began to race and she could almost feel someone running up behind her. She felt trapped; she felt scared and she felt Pete. She looked back down through the Window, her hand on her chest. She was sensing Pete's terror, his pain, and she was going to stop it. Right now.

Shye could see that Veil's attention was now fully on Pete and as her eyes widened, he too shifted his focus downward, zooming in on Pete's attack. He could see the two men kicking him, could hear that he was screaming in pain and panic. The beer was spilt all over the pavement. Shye's heart sank, knowing there was nothing they could do. Veil was going to be heartbroken that Pete was getting hurt, but it was not their time to save people; it was their time to stay out of the way and let things run their course. As he turned to console his friend, Veil was already moving away, unstoppable and unwavering in her decision. The breeze was blowing her robe around her legs and she reached for the pendant on her chest, ready to unleash her wings. Shye and Dusk exchanged quick glances, both pairs of eyes panic-stricken as they ran to her. They grabbed her arms, trying to restrain her. She was pushing and thrashing as hard as she could against them, her face feral as she began screaming.

"Please no, Veil! Calm down!!" Shye was shouting and pleading with her but her incredible strength continued to pull them all forward, towards the Window.

"Pete is in trouble! LET ME GO!! I have to go!" Veil screamed as she struggled to free herself from them.

Dusk shouted this time, trying to reason with her. "You can't go down there! Not at night. Come on, think, Veil! The Draxyls outnumber you a hundred to one!! We'll ask Sol what to do! Don't…"

23

Veil broke free and ran as fast as she could, her friends unable to keep up, or stop her, as she leapt through the gap. Shye tried to reach out and grab her, but she was a few steps ahead and he almost followed her down through the Window. As she began to fall, she grabbed her wings pendant hanging around her neck and smacked it hard against her chest. Within a second of bright light, her glorious wings unfurled, as she dove towards Earth to rescue Pete. Her wings were not as big as Shye's, but every bit as impressive, each feather shining silver, like her eyes, a slight tint of purple at the tip. As she fell, she briefly looked back up to the Window and saw Shye reaching down in terror. She returned her gaze to the street she was aiming for. As she grew closer, she opened her wings and directed herself east, then slowly made her descent. She was just a few metres above the street, and in those last few seconds, everything slowed almost to a pause as she aimed her feet with perfect precision.

Her feet hit the floor so hard she made a large crack in the pavement. A moment after landing, and despite the onlookers, she reached up for her wings pendant and hit her chest again, her large purple tinged wings slowly retreating into her back as she surveyed the scene in front of her. Pete was on the floor. He appeared to be unconscious, yet the two ferocious looking men continued to kick him. Tears began to prickle her eyes as she surveyed the scene; only for a moment though. A flicker of her powerful heart reminded her: she was a Guardian and she would, therefore, guard with every fibre of her being and every feather of her wings. She was no warrior—she wasn't as fast as Dusk, or as strong as Shye—but in that moment she felt unstoppable, driven onward by the need to inflict pain on those inflicting it on Pete.

She ran as fast as she could towards the larger man standing over Pete's head, kicking him in the face. Her head hit him first, with all of her force aimed at his mid-section, and it threw him backwards at least ten feet. He tumbled onto the black wet road, somersaulting head over heels several times before coming to a stop. The other assailant stopped his kicking and stepped forward, thrusting his right fist at Veil, which she blocked easily and grabbed him by the throat, lifting him a foot above the pavement. She looked into his face, his light hair rain-slicked against it. He hissed loudly, like a rattlesnake under threat. Holding onto his neck, she bent her elbow and threw him as hard as she could. He went high into the air and crashed down into a fruit stand across the street. Veil looked down at Pete: he seemed so vulnerable and small, bruised and battered and soaked through because of the rain. She was preparing herself to lift him away from this chaos, when she suddenly felt a sharp pain at the back of her head, her knees buckled and the street began to spin. She tried to focus on the men she had thrown, walking towards her now, with cruel, victorious smiles on their faces.

Veil fell to the floor not far from Pete. She tried to stand but then she felt someone's foot hit her back, knocking her to the pavement again. Then a fist connected with her jaw, completely disorientating her, and she cried out in pain, immediately tasting blood. It was on the delivery of this blow that Veil realised: whoever was attacking her was stronger than she was, and with this thought came panic. She turned her head just enough to look upon her attackers; three of them. Where had the third person come from? Then she saw it. The largest of the three turned again towards Pete and she saw the tattoo on his neck: a swift V shape with a mark underneath it—a mark of darkness. Dusk's warning rang loud in her head.

"The Draxyls outnumber you a hundred to one."

It was a trap. Someone had hurt Pete to trap her, she realised, in spite of the throbbing in her head. A cloud of guilt and pain descended around her and she stopped fighting the blows that inevitably continued to strike. She just lay there, receiving blow after blow. The Draxyls were going to win; there would be more of them on the way and she didn't stand a chance—these were the unforgiving facts that now filled her mind. She was going to die, along with Pete, on a cold, wet pavement, and no other Guardians would fly down, knowing it was suicide. The Knights of the Sun would not come to her rescue. Sol wouldn't sacrifice them for the sake of her stupidity. She was alone.

Veil felt herself being rolled onto her back by the toe of a shoe; she looked up into the three vicious faces of the Draxyls. It was raining harder now, and she had to keep blinking in order to renew her sight. The man she had run at looked like a punk, with his blue and black hair sticking up in every direction and his black eyes outlined in black eye make-up. His lips were curled back, revealing razor-sharp teeth, multiple piercings in his ears, nose and lower lip, sinister and shining. The smaller man, whom Veil had successfully thrown across a street, had long, stringy blonde hair hanging down the side of his pale face, so expressionless and empty. She finally saw the woman—the one who must have hit her from behind. Her face was so sharp it almost had pointed edges. Her skin was the colour of milk and her eyes, unlike the others, were dark silver and as shiny as mirror glass. All this was framed by deep red hair with black tips, and her black torn clothes smelled of smoke.

A loud clap of thunder erupted above them, simultaneous with a bright flash of lightning, and it began pouring with harsh, painful rain. The rain seemed angry and violent, like it was yelling at someone, and each drop that struck Veil's face felt like a small wet bullet. The Draxyls all looked up to the sky, the rain hitting their faces. Veil watched in fear and hopelessness, as they all smiled towards the heavens, before turning their attention back to her. She thought she must have been going crazy, because the more she concentrated on the girl with red hair, the more the girl began to look like her. Things around her were growing dark, yet the girl now looked like her own reflection, her red hair turned to dark brown, the purple hints appearing, now *her* face and *her* eyes. Her own hand was reaching out for her...Veil succumbed to the darkness.

Pete stirred and pulled himself up onto his knees, his head bowed as he coughed with the effort, trying to shift the pain pushing his chest down. As he recovered from his coughing fit, he looked up and saw his attackers crowded around his defender. He could barely see what was unfolding before him, the rain coming down harder than he had ever seen or felt, the tiny drops hitting him with such ferocity he was sure he would be covered in a thousand tiny bruises. Not knowing what came over him, and almost on an automatic response, he reached for the beer cans that he had dropped during his assault and hurled them as far as he could without any real aim—just the hope of the right outcome. The beer hit the big guy's head and then fell to the floor. With a sudden whoosh, the cans split open and beer began spraying up, drenching the attackers looming over the unconscious girl. The two big guys scowled at Pete and began running towards him, hands outstretched menacingly, when another lightning bolt flew overhead. They stopped in their tracks, for a moment glaring at Pete with ominous focus, and then ran away in the rain. Pete turned his attention to the woman left standing, the rain now coming down so hard that he couldn't make out any real distinguishing features, just that she had long dark hair and wore a long dress. The silhouette reached down and grabbed something from the neck of her unconscious victim, then reached up to her own neck. Pete continued to watch in amazement until a bright flash of gold stole all of his vision, and he raised his hand in front of his face to shield his eyes. When finally he could see again, the female assailant was gone and there was only a figure on the floor.

Pete immediately rushed to her side and brushed the wet hair back from her face. The rain had eased off significantly and was now no more than a gently spray, washing over the girl's heavily bruised right cheek, mingling with the blood trickling from the small gash under her chin. She was still going to become ill unless he got her inside soon. With all of the strength he had left in him, Pete gently lifted the beaten girl, cradling her in his arms as if she were a child who had fallen off her bike. The thunder and lightning had now faded into the distance, leaving only a chill in the air and an eerie quiet on the street. With unsteady steps and shaking arms, Pete began walking; he was not far from home. As he carried the unconscious girl—his defender—he breathed in deeply, taking in her scent. He recognised it instantly: lavender. He smiled and carried her away in the rain.

Chapter Four

Dusk and Shye were still at the Window, where a crowd had begun to gather at the news of Veil's descent to Earth at night and in the pouring rain. A mix of worry and anxiety filled everyone's faces, none more so than Shye's. He had rallied together a select few members of the League of Guardians: the strongest and most fearless. Yet, as he observed the crowd, he saw no brave faces, or willing volunteers to bring back their sister and friend: he saw only fear and reluctance. As he sought the eyes of an ally, his gaze came to rest upon Kin, who always gave the illusion of being smaller and more fragile than the other Guardians.

Shye considered Kin carefully as he looked through the Window. He appeared terrified and confused and although his size was almost as impressive as his own, Shye knew his friend was special. Kin did not believe his intelligence, speed and strength measured up to that of the other Guardians. His wings were neither as wide nor as glorious; his mousey brown hair and light brown eyes were quite bland compared to the features of some of the others, and Shye knew this saddened his friend greatly. Whilst he was observing Kin, and simultaneously pondered a rescue mission, he felt a soft hand grip his. He didn't need to turn around; he could sense Dusk behind him, could feel her smile through the clothes on his back.

"What are we going to do?" he asked aloud, preparing himself for reassurance that did not come.

"Nothing."

Shye spun around so fast that he knocked her hand away with his action. She looked at him, stunned. He had such anger and disbelief in his eyes; it was a look she had never wanted to receive from him. A red, hostile energy radiated from him, and he began to tremble, challenging her with his intimidating presence. Neither had noticed, but his rapid change in mood and sudden movement had drawn all attention to them. A single tear rolled down Dusk's cheek; she quickly and angrily wiped it away. She took a step forward and, standing on tiptoes, looked him right in the eye. No fear or surrender, she spoke in a voice that was firm and just loud enough so that their audience could hear it.

"Shye, do not reflect your anger onto me. We tried to stop Veil and she wouldn't listen to reason. The rain was coming down so hard during her attack that no one could see the outcome. No one, Shye, and you and I were right there.

"We have no way of knowing if she can be saved, and no way of knowing how many Draxyls are down there, or even if any were involved. We can not lead a team into the dark when we can't be sure that we could return. There are a million and more reasons why we shouldn't fly down there and I don't have the time to give, nor you the patience to hear them right now. But above all there is one damned good reason why we do not fly to Earth at night and Veil knew that as well as any of us do. Night is Vulgaar's time and it becomes his domain. He has an infinite number of Draxyls on his side. No amount of good intention or Guardians is a match for them. I couldn't bear the thought of you going down there and...not coming back." Dusk had spoken in a calm clear voice and now looked directly into his eyes; she could see they were softening. "Please don't be angry with me," she finished, barely above a whisper.

The words made Shye's heart break a little and he nodded in understanding, smiling gently. He reached out his hand; she took it and they linked fingers, each relishing in the soft and comforting contact. They both regarded the group around them; many had dispersed during their discussion, for fear of being called upon to act. Shye gave them all the same nod he had given Dusk. They would wait.

Just as they had stilled and quietly returned to watching through the Window, they saw a shape emerging through the rain and heading up towards them. Fast. They all looked closer and Shye made his way through the crowd to be at the Window's edge, pulling Dusk by the hand. Kin had moved himself to the back of the group, hiding behind the others, peeking through the gaps between the vast number of heads. The figure appeared to be a woman, but it was impossible to say for sure, only outlined by rain, and whoever it was didn't have wings. The flying shadow was almost at the Window now; Shye and Dusk stood back and motioned for everyone to do the same. Nothing happened, but all continued watching anxiously, hands over their hearts and pendants. Shye was breathing heavily as his mind considered the lack of incident, his eyes narrowing sceptically.

All of a sudden, a huge flash of light erupted from the Window and the woman shot through like a bullet, straight up into the air. Everyone watched, as she flew upwards, becoming an undistinguishable, small blur high above their heads. Then she began to fall, her legs and arms flailing around like a parachuter who had forgotten to pull the cord. As she got closer, Shye and Dusk both thought they recognised her and Shye beamed with hope. When they realised where she would land, they all manoeuvred quickly, creating a circle, and she dropped, full force, into the middle of it. She didn't move; she just lay on her side with her head resting on her forearm, her dark purple hair covering her face and neck. Shye let go of Dusk's hand and began moving forward slowly, his arm up and hand gesturing for everyone to remain where they were. As he got closer something bothered him; he didn't know what, but he had an uneasy feeling. It was mainly that he couldn't smell anything, no rain, or Earth, or lavender. He was close enough now to touch her, and noticed she was dripping wet and shivering. He slowly reached his hand to touch her shoulder, not wanting to scare or hurt her. As his fingertips made a feather-like contact with her right shoulder, the girl abruptly turned over and looked straight into his eyes.

"Veil?"

Chapter Five

Veil felt pain—a hot searing pain in her face and the lower half of her back when she tried to move. She attempted rolling to her left and felt pain, to her right and felt more pain, so she gave up and remained still, on her back. Whatever she was lying on wasn't helping matters; it was cold and lumpy with far too many blankets weighing her down. This was strange, because she didn't sleep with blankets and her bed was always warm. She slowly opened one eye—her left eye that didn't hurt—and scanned the room. Very carefully, she opened her other eye. It hurt like hell. She took everything in. She was lying in a bed that was far bigger than her own—a double, with mismatched quilts and patchwork blankets, all ruffled over her legs. There were big windows on the left side of the room, so big they reached floor to ceiling, creating the illusion that the far wall was made up entirely of the skyline. On the nearest wall was a mounted small flat-screen television with a DVD player underneath and a stereo under that. There were modest potted plants in two corners of the room and artistic black and white photographs on every wall, although none of them together; scattered around. Fragmented. Many of them were shots of the sky or beach. She observed the computer desk by the door, resting on it a sizeable monitor and white keyboard, surrounded by papers and old coffee mugs.

She tried to move again, but was met with unpleasant achiness throughout her body and she was moving so slowly. Too slowly, she really didn't like it. She pushed herself up into a sitting position using her hands and cast her eyes down to her body. She was wearing a shirt; it was blue, the buttons fastened into the wrong buttonholes, and it was far too big for her. It smelled wonderful, like oranges, and felt soft against her skin. Her eyebrows drew in confusion, as she tried frantically to remember the events of the previous evening, but she could only recall the rain, and the sound of thunder. She thought back to her friends; she thought of Shye, and Dusk, and Kin, and tried to recall their last conversation. And then it hit her, like a hammer to the head: falling through the Window and looking back at Shye's face. Guilt and fear ripped through her. She had no idea where she was. She heard footsteps approaching the bedroom.

She grabbed the blankets around her legs and pulled them to cover her body, wincing in pain as she did so. The door squeaked slightly as it opened, and a head peaked around to look at her. Veil's eyes opened in surprise and she felt the happiness wash over her as she took in the features of Pete Standon. He looked at her with such concern and wonderment that she felt her heart melt. He entered the room carrying a tray of food and a glass of orange juice; he was limping and sporting an ugly purple and black bruise on his neck, but otherwise he looked fine, although Veil still felt guilty, knowing he was probably hurt because Draxyls were setting a trap for her. She watched him closely through eyes masked with sadness.

"I'm sorry. Did I wake you?" he asked, Veil closed her eyes, letting his voice wash over her and calm her. It was soft and yet masculine; she already felt safe. So overcome with emotion, she didn't trust her own voice, so she just slowly shook her head in response.

"Well," Pete began, "I'm Dr. Peter Standon and you're at my apartment. How much of last night can you remember?" He tilted his head slightly to the right in a questioning yet sympathetic manner, watching closely for a reaction. Veil could only remember as far back as hurling the Draxyls away from Pete, and then everything went blank.

"I...ummm..." Getting her bearings she tried the direct answer. "I remember it was raining. I remember you were being attacked and I did my best to help." At this she carefully watched Pete's face to see if he believed this story, that was at the very least leaving out massive amounts of detail. "And I can remember you were unconscious, and then I woke up here, in your bed, in your apartment and...in your shirt?"

Pete laughed at this assessment. Veil was caught offguard by that laugh; she knew he wasn't being mean. It was a gentle laugh that made his whole face light up. Veil decided she liked this laugh. She liked it a lot and inexplicably laughed along with him. Once the giggles had subsided, Pete spoke again.

"Well, my version of events is probably just as vague. I was having a traumatic enough day yesterday, even before my little tumble on the pavement. Have you seen anything on the news about the fire at Raphael's Hospital?"

Veil bit her tongue about being there, he would find out eventually anyway, so again she simply nodded. Pete nodded back and continued with his story.

"I'm a doctor at Raphael's and tried to help people out of the hallways yesterday." He paused and took a deep breath. It was obviously still too raw to talk about and Veil was almost overwhelmed by the desire to hug him and kiss his cheek to comfort him.

"Anyway, last night I was feeling low and stopped to get some beer, which means I must have been in a sorry state because I very rarely drink. This huge guy began following me, and his little friend too, and the next thing I know I'm on the floor trying to fight them off, but they kept kicking me in the head and pushing their feet into my back. I think I must have blacked out from exhaustion, or fear. Either way, the next time I opened my eyes, you were on the floor surrounded by them and I didn't even think about what I was doing. I just wanted them to stop hurting you!" He was nearly shouting now and Veil grinned at his protective streak coming through and glowed inside and out, knowing it was for her.

Pete began pacing the bedroom and gesturing wildly as he recounted the next part of the events.

"So I picked up the six pack I dropped when they jumped me and hurled it at the big guy hoping to knock him out or something, but the weird thing is it just," Pete clapped his hands together, "bounced right off his huge gross head and then onto the floor, shooting the beer up into their faces."

Veil laughed, wishing she had been conscious to see that. But her laughter died when she caught the look in Pete's eyes, as if he didn't want to tell her the rest. He looked slightly embarrassed.

"Then what happened, Pete?"

Pete cleared his throat and looked at his hands before he continued.

"Please don't think me crazy," he implored, "but I swear there was a huge crack of thunder and the rain came down so hard and so fast that I couldn't see you and then a blinding light surrounded you. I thought you had been struck by lightning and then they were gone and you were alone. So I picked you up and carried you here, because the hospital was still inaccessible. I checked you out...I mean over!"

They both shared an almost cheeky smile and Veil could feel her cheeks burning red.

"Ummm...yeah, so you just have a few nasty bruises on your ribs, but they'll feel better in a couple of days. You had a slight concussion but I checked your pupils just before you woke up and they seem OK now. You don't appear to have a fever, although you are very warm, and I think the tattoo on your back is amazing."

Pete whispered the last part, but Veil didn't feel complimented. She felt panic. Was she now a Draxyl?

"Ya know—your wings? On your back? That must've taken hours and I love the purple tint they have. It's gorgeous and very unique." Pete continued to gush, but Veil still seemed confused. She reached up to her neck, round her chest and frantically began searching through her hair.

"Have you seen my necklace?" she asked quickly.

Pete just stared at her.

"My necklace? It has wings on it? Where is it?!" she shouted, thinking that Pete had simply removed it when examining her.

"I'm sorry but I don't recall ever seeing one. I carried you here and undressed you and never saw one." His voice was full of guilt; he should have looked for her personal belongings before he brought her back here. Veil was crying, Pete gently sat on the bed next to her.

"Hey, it's OK. We'll look for it when we're both well enough, OK? I've just realised I don't know your name. It's very hard to comfort someone when they're nameless."

Veil looked straight into his eyes and saw nothing but sincerity and concern there, so she followed her heart.

"My name is Veil."

Pete gasped and took in her hair. It looked different now than it had last night, when it had been slightly damp from the downpour. He leaned slightly closer to her and sniffed, then leaned a little closer and sniffed deeper, like a dog at a fellow dog. Veil looked at him quizzically.

"Lavender," Pete said, grinning. "You were at the hospital?"

Veil nodded meekly but wasn't feeling up to elaborating, which Pete must have sensed, as he too just gave a little nod.

"Well, Veil," he said as he laid a hand on her shoulder, "I'm very glad you came to my rescue last night. Tomorrow we will search for your necklace, and with any luck not run into those creeps again. Let's just hope they got whatever it was that they wanted." He looked at her hopefully. She slowly raised her head, her eyes dark as she answered.

"Let's not."

Chapter Six

Back in Aureia, Shye was kneeling next to Veil with a look of concern on his face. She wasn't hurt, or didn't appear to be; she was just wet and very cold. He could see she was breathing and her wings pendant was around her neck. He gently shook her; the Guardians crowded around, mumbling their distress and fear among themselves. Kin watched on silently as the scene unfolded, his eyes never leaving Shye and Veil on the ground.

"Veil? Can you hear me? It's Shye." He gently wiped wet hair from her face as he spoke.

She stirred but didn't open her eyes, her face turned towards him, scrunched up like she was in pain. When Shye was granted that look at her face he gasped. She was so pale and sickly. She opened her eyes—dark purple, her pupils were fully dilated and seemed to zero in on Shye's face. For that brief instant, Shye felt no familiarity for this girl and it scared him. She quickly covered her eyes with her hand and cried out.

"Agh! It's too bright! Why is it so bright?! Turn the lights off or something!"

Even her voice didn't sound right. Shye really began to worry that something traumatic had happened to his friend and he was kicking himself for not following her through the Window. She was thrashing against him and rolling around as if in agony. He tried to restrain her arms, fearing she would injure herself, but his efforts were proving futile, his huge arms struggling to control her frantic movements, whilst she continued to wail, now even louder, about the light hurting her eyes.

"Kin! Come help me! NOW!" he shouted.

Kin immediately ran to his friend's aid and grabbed Veil's feet. She was kicking with such force he looked for Dusk to also assist. She didn't hesitate and soon others were putting their hands on the writhing body in an effort to calm her, each Guardian whispering words of encouragement and comfort, but to no avail. There were twelve people and twenty-four sets of hands trying to still the erratic girl who was strangely becoming dry from all the movement. She was now moving so quickly that it was difficult to see her as more than just a blur of motion. Then suddenly she stopped; completely stopped. Every part of her body was still, apart from her chest, heaving out long, heavy breaths. Her eyes were closed but it was obvious she was concentrating. She began to tremble slightly and Shye felt what was becoming before it actually happened but he didn't have time to react, because within a blink of an eye they all went flying in different directions.

Veil pushed them all away, up in the air with her mere energy. It was as if it were in slow motion, and Shye hung in the air looking around him at everyone else, arms flaying around and panic in their eyes. They fell with heavy thuds to the ground, and some cried out in pain as their bodies collided hard with the floor. Shye was the first to stand up; he quickly looked to the others to ensure no one was seriously injured and once he had made a satisfactory assessment, he returned his attention to Veil. Kin helped Dusk from the floor and the other Guardians stood and slowly turned their attention to Veil. Everyone was shocked and astonished by the event that had just taken place. No Guardian possessed that kind of power and it frightened them all. Now the group that had previously tried to restrain her formed a large circle around her, keeping their distance and now far greater in number, so there was in effect, a wall of Guardians surrounding her body.

Shye took a step forward, Dusk watching on with trepidation in her eyes, fearing for his safety. He was a few feet from her now, and felt everyone's eyes following his slow movements. As he approached, Veil appeared to be asleep, still breathing rapidly, her eyes closed. Shye surmised that she was in shock. He reached out with his hand as he was going to attempt shaking her awake and took a step closer, noticing that her breathing had slowed, she had stopped trembling and her eyelids were twitching as if she were about to open her eyes. His fingers were almost on her when she abruptly sat upright and her eyes flung wide open, the movement causing Shye to jump back. Everyone gasped in surprise and Kin too was startled by the action though he was the furthest one away. Veil's head raised and she took in everyone's faces slowly, staring into their eyes until they felt as though she were looking right through them. Her face was lifeless, her hair dark and dull, but the most disturbing part of her appearance was her eyes. They had changed colour, no longer vibrant with life and although they were still purple, it was such a dark purple that it was almost black and there was something eerily alien about them, like they were seeing everything for the first time. She jumped into a crouch, her hands holding her body and her knees bent near her chin. She kept her head down slightly, dark hair falling in front of her eyes, peering through the straggly strands as she focused her attention on Shye, whose expression remained one of curiosity and concern.

Her eyes narrowed, searching his face, looking for something familiar, yet this person was clean, bright and warm, and distinctly unknown to her. He was looking at her—really looking at her; like a friend, the distress and love emanating from him in waves. She wasn't sure if she was comfortable under such scrutiny; no one had ever looked at her like this before.

"Veil?" he asked again. She appeared to be taking him in and he was frightened. What had happened to her down there? He continued slowly edging forward. Lash suddenly remembered this was supposed to be her name—Veil. She nodded so he knew she could hear him.

"Do you know where you are?"

She nodded again. Pleased with the responses he continued.

"Are you hurt?"

She shook her head to indicate no. Everyone breathed a sigh of relief.

"Is there anything you need?"

At this she fully lifted her head and relaxed her posture a little, no longer feeling she was in danger. She looked right into the stranger's eyes and nodded again, smiling. He smiled back and held out his hand to her. For a moment she examined it suspiciously, then looked into his face again and accepted it.

Chapter Seven

Before she could attempt sleep, Veil went to Pete's bathroom, to inspect the tattoo he'd spoken of. The bathroom was small, modest, yet oddly spacious, with only a small bath tub with a shower overhead and shiny taps that reflected the room around them, distorting it like a funhouse mirror. The little sink had a mirrored medicine cabinet above it, which held the image of about half of Veil's body. She inspected her face: the bruising had faded some and she was bearing only a small purple bruise around her eye now. Otherwise she looked fine; she looked like herself. She made a thorough inspection of her eyes: they were still purple, not black or red, which she felt immensely relieved about; in fact, although they were definitely still purple, they had actually lightened in colour, making them appear more vibrant and alive. She took a deep breath and slowly turned around.

She inspected her neck and back, gently pulling her long purple hair away with her hand so that it now hung down her right shoulder. Her neck bore no tattoo; it was just creamy white skin, and she sighed in relief to know she wasn't wearing the mark of a Draxyl. On her back however, the expanse of skin was completely covered with an incredibly detailed and precise ink copy of the wings deep in her skin; very much like a tattoo. They were perfect; they ran from the top of her shoulder blades right to the base of her back. The tops were wide and bold, sloping down in a deep curve, and the ends were pointed but didn't look sharp. They possessed easily over 10,000 feathers, each one silver flecked with purple.

Veil smiled. These were her new wings; wings that couldn't expand and make her fly, but reminded her of home and who she was. As her gaze drifted along the curve of her left wing, she noticed some of the wing appeared to be missing. Not much at all, but Veil could see that five or six of her feathers had faded. She frowned and made a mental note to herself to ask Pete if he had noticed, then walked back to his bedroom, passing his sleeping form on the sofa. She crawled back into his bed and tried to sleep, her mind filling with thoughts of how she was going to retrieve her wings tomorrow, and how much the pillow smelled like Pete.

Pete had kept his word: after a restless night of little sleep, followed by a breakfast in bed, consisting of bagels, cream cheese and orange juice—which made Veil smile all morning and almost forget about her missing wings—they headed back for the street where they were attacked. Veil had borrowed some of Pete's clothes; they were very big and the shirt she was wearing looked like a nightgown, but they smelled like Pete and that made her happy. As they approached the spot on the street, Veil began to feel uneasy. She kept looking for something familiar to pinpoint where the fight had occurred but she was having only flashbacks of the darkness and feeling scared. Sensing her discomfort, Pete laid his hand on her elbow to gently nudge her in the right direction and she instantly felt better. She put her hand on his, keeping it in place.

"Are you sure you're up to this?" he asked, his brow creased in concern. Veil had noticed he did that a lot and she didn't like him worrying. She smiled up at him, observing his eyes brighten a little.

"Yes. Honestly, Pete, I'm fine. I just need to find my necklace."

Now they both realised they were standing in the exact spot where everything had happened. It looked like a typical street in a very normal area of the small city. Veil glanced up to a high point on one of the brick buildings as they walked, where 'Bank Street' was printed on a small plaque. The street itself had grey pavements with faded chewing gum marks, pigeons doddering about nearby and people mingling, shopping and talking. Veil and Pete let go of one another, but remained facing each other, just soaking in their surroundings. By the light of day, the street seemed so ordinary and unthreatening. Dozens of people walked around them, happily going about their business, oblivious to the events that had taken place the previous evening. The whole area looked so different in the daylight, although they still scanned the buildings, people, trees at eye level, to make sure they were safe. When it became apparent to them that they were, they began examining the pavement, searching for Veil's 'necklace'. Pete looked up from the ground.

"What does it look like?"

"Hmmm," she said, struggling to create a visual description. "Well, it's got a long silver chain, kind of thick and heavy." She began to smile as she continued; "On the end of the chain is a pendant in the shape of wings. They're beautiful—not very big, but they shine all the time and have a tiny hint of purple at the end of each feather." As she described them, she began to think about how they felt; they gave her power and strength. When she had them against her chest she felt special and connected to something so great and magical that she considered herself lucky every day she wore them. But then her smile faded as she was overcome by feelings of sadness and hopelessness, sensing she already knew where they were—around a Draxyl's neck.

"It's very important to me," she said. She turned her face towards the ground and a single tear left her eye. Pete nodded in understanding and got on his hands and knees in order to better view the ground. Veil watched him, with his bottom in the air and his face close to ground, crawling frantically in circles around her. He looked like a puppy sniffing for treats, and then began to sniff like a dog. He sniffed her shoes, then her legs, just like a dog finding something interesting. She smiled down at him and tucked her purple hair behind her ear. Seeing that he'd succeeded in making her smile, he continued and began to make a yapping noise like a puppy, until she was laughing out loud and so hard that tears had sprung to her eyes. He stood up and started to laugh too, and soon they were both doubled over with laughter, gasping for air and wiping tears from their eyes.

They were facing each other now, each enjoying the sound of the other's laughter, and as it quietened down they found that they were gazing warmly into each other's faces, smiles on their lips, both taking this opportunity to really see each other. Veil looked into Pete's eyes—deep brown with flecks of honey. She knew he was tired, and yet they were so vibrant and she sensed his appreciation as he looked upon her. His nose was straight, his lips full and kind of long so that when he smiled they stretched right across his face. He had a little stubble, which she knew, from years of watching him, was a new style; it looked soft and was the colour of his hair—a sandy brown. In Veil's eyes he was the most beautiful man and she felt privileged to be looking on him so closely.

Pete, in turn, was also holding Veil's face under inspection. He noticed she was pale, but not at all like his sick patients in the hospital. She was a very pretty pale, like a china doll. Her eyes—he'd never seen anyone with eyes that colour before—they were beautiful and bright, almost lavender. He smiled to himself at this thought—lavender—and continued his inspection. No wrinkles or frown lines; no marks or blemishes. Her skin was flawless, bar the bruise on her cheek, and her nose was slender, like the kind he'd seen on super models. Her lips were magnificent; red and full with a well defined Cupid's bow on her top lip. Her hair flowed over her shoulders and covered most of back, and it was very dark but with a very prominent hint of purple visible in the sunshine. He couldn't help thinking how soft it looked and he momentarily wanted to reach out and stroke it.

A passerby accidentally bumped into Pete, breaking the spell. He and Veil both smiled awkwardly and cast their eyes downward to carry on the search, she to the left, he to the right. As Veil scoured one patch of pavement after another, she began to feel dizzy and discouraged. It all looked just the same. She heard the small tinkle of a bell and a door opening and closing; it was the store she had witnessed Pete leaving the night before. She walked on a little further and then she smelled it: beer. She looked down and saw a wet patch on the concrete, drying in the sun; it was the beer that Pete had thrown to save her. She crouched on the balls of her feet and scanned the small area, gasping when she saw drops of blood, dark crimson in colour. She knew they belonged to Pete and herself, and it made her shiver. She searched frantically, checked every crack, every crevice but it was no use. She couldn't find her wings, which meant she couldn't get home. She looked up into the sunshine, thought of home and her friends, and began to cry.

Chapter Eight

The Guardians were gathered around Veil, listening intently as she regaled them with her magnificent tale of being on Earth in the dark and during a storm. They were fascinated by her bravery and the way she spoke of saving Pete and vanquishing the Draxyls. As she talked, her voice and actions became more animated, she was almost frantic and the Guardians watching her seemed to be enjoying her story all the more for it.

"Then just as I was about to lift Pete from the ground," she told them, "this sneaky little Draxyl with red hair gave me a flying kick right in the back of my head, and I smacked down to the ground. BANG!" She clapped her hands together emphasising the noise, startling the avid listeners around her. She gave a small satisfied smirk and continued.

"I was down on the floor, weak and pathetic. I mean really, *really* feeble. I was crawling along the pavement, begging for my life and crying my eyes out—seriously guys, if you had seen what a coward I was being you would've hated me. Anyway, the rain started coming down harder and harder, so hard it was stinging my face. I was surrounded; there were at least fifty of those ugly buggers, all just laughing at me as I pathetically tried to crawl to Pete, God, he's a loser. He was even more useless than I was! Then just when I thought we were done for…"

Lash took a long pause and looked through the crowd. Everyone was rapt, completely enthralled, their eyes brimming with excitement and anticipation, like a classroom filled with children listening to a story. They even began to lean forward, trying to convey how much they wanted her to go on. Stupid cloud riders, she thought, This'll scare them. She had a quiet laugh to herself and then carried on in a quiet tone.

"But then I heard this rumbling from above me. The sky was—growling. The dirty Draxyls all looked up and began laughing hysterically, all crazy like. Then all of a sudden, the growling stopped and then there was an enormous CRASH!" She nearly screamed the last part, once again making her audience jump with fright.

"From above us was a huge ball of fire, and thunder and lightning all at once. It was the scariest thing I have ever seen, and bright and hot! It was there for a couple of minutes, then poof! It was gone again and so were the Draxyls. It was just me and Pete lying in the rain, beaten up. We both got up, he went home, I came here. The end." She finished her story with a big smile on her face as she took in the horrified expressions of the Guardians around her. A lot of them were very pale and some looked as though they might cry.

Dusk and Shye were watching from a distance. They too had heard her story and were both confused and anxious. They could also see the evident fear on the Guardians' faces, particularly Kin, who was well known for being a little skittish anyway. He had shrunk away from the crowd and now stood alone at the back of them; he appeared to be shaking. Dusk and Shye continued to watch Veil and her movements. Even her manner of speaking seemed alien to them, her hand gestures, the way her whole body animated as she spoke. They always recalled Veil as being calm and composed when she spoke or told stories. Shye was the first to break the silence.

"Well, that was interesting," he said quietly to Dusk.

"Yes, I had no idea she was so...so...excited? What do you think is wrong with her? Trauma from the encounter?"

"No. I did at first, but did you hear how she spoke of Pete? And the way she was insulting herself? Calling herself a coward and feeble? That's not the Veil we know. Maybe Vulgaar has used magic on her?"

"Maybe," Dusk agreed thoughtfully. "We should keep an eye on her. Perhaps consult Sol? See what she thinks?"

As Dusk said Sol's name, Veil's head quickly snapped in their direction. They both smiled politely, a little shaken that she seemed to have heard their conversation. They continued in whispers.

"No," Shye said, "I won't go to her yet. I'm sure she'll speak to me if she needs to."

Lash grinned as she watched, listening intently to their conversation. *Sol speaks to Shye? Then I'll just have to be there when she does.*

Shye returned his attention to Veil and saw her looking at him, a curved, mischievous grin on her face. Her wings looked sick and they were twitching. He had noticed the purple in them had faded dramatically and feathers had fallen out. Also peculiar was the fact that she wasn't retracting them. They were constantly on her back, on display, making their small nervous convulsions from time to time, like now. And even though there were no clouds or shadows in Aureia, as Shye looked upon Veil, he could see darkness all around her.

Chapter Nine

Shye had been walking alone for a long time, away from the group and close to Unenda. He was hoping that by being away from them Sol would appear and talk to him. Well, not appear—he'd never seen her, but over the past few years she'd spoken to him a handful of times when he was in trouble and had no guide. He wasn't pacing, just wandering slowly, aimlessly, head bowed, his hair hanging loose around his face and shoulders, his grey eyes barely concealing his concern under eyebrows drawn as he tried to concentrate, listening for a sign, a sound. Suddenly he felt a chill and a presence near him and lifted his head; he slowly turned around. Veil was standing there, one leg bent at the knee in front of the other, her hands behind her back and her head tilted coyly to the side as she studied Shye from head to toe. He felt uncomfortable under such scrutiny; Veil had never looked at him like this before.

"I've been looking for you everywhere," she said.

"Well, I just needed some time alone, to think."

She smiled and started walking slowly towards him. Her wings were twitching again; she was making him nervous.

"Hmmm," she said, "and just who were you thinking about?"

Why would she ask that? he thought to himself; she was acting very strangely.

"No one in particular," Shye answered. "Just thinking

about Aureia. Did you need me?" He was backing away from her.

"More than you know," she shot back. "You're very impressive, Shye. I don't know why I've never seen it before. How tall, handsome, strong and good you are." She held his gaze.

Shye didn't like this. Veil wasn't like this. She didn't think these things about him.

"Veil? Are you OK? I mean, did you hit your head or something?" He laughed a little at the question, trying to lighten the mood. It was getting too intense. She continued to advance, shaking her head from side to side in an exaggerated fashion.

"I'm fine, Shye, it's just—I don't know. When I was down there and Pete was being all weak and pathetic and human, all I could think was, 'I wish Shye were here.' And here you are. Shouldn't we make the most of it?"

As she'd been talking she'd come very close to him. Shye and the imposter were nearly toe to toe, though he was much taller than she was. At this distance, he could really examine her face and eyes. Her usually flawless skin had tiny yet visible veins manifesting around the sides of her face. She looked so pale and her cheeks were no longer flushed; her lips were dry and cracked, and her eyes, while still purple, seemed lifeless. They were much darker, with small flecks of red in them and dark circles had appeared underneath them. Likewise, her hair, while also still purple, appeared greasy and unkempt. However, the most troubling thing of all to Shye was that his friend had been home for two days now and had yet to retract her wings. They were hanging low on her back and it looked as though the feathers had continued to fall out. The white parts of her wings were a dirty brown-grey colour and the tips were so pale, no longer that vibrant, noticeable purple.

Also, with her this close, Shye failed to smell lavender, which had always been her signature smell. Now all he could smell was Earth after the rain, and smoke.

He was becoming increasingly concerned for his friend; this behaviour was so out of character that he was no longer sure it was even her. She was staring at him, with such a strange smile on her face, one he had never seen before. Veil's smiles were usually so big and bright, and reserved just for watching Pete. Suddenly she reached for his face, touched his cheek and then began stroking his hair. Shye recoiled from her hand. It was cold and the tips of her fingers were rough and cracked and felt like tree bark against his skin. He shook his head at her and frowned, confused and appalled by her behaviour. The imposter was quite hurt by his actions; did he not find 'Veil' attractive? What was wrong with her?

"What's your problem?" she asked harshly, taking a step away from him.

"What's yours?" he countered. "Ever since you've been back you've been acting strangely. Now this? This isn't you, Veil. You're a good Guardian and you always have good intentions. I mean, for God's sake, you only got yourself into this mess because you dove to Earth without any hesitation to save Pete!" Shye was shouting now, and the girl posing as Veil was watching him closely and curiously as he continued.

"And why haven't you retracted your wings yet? Why haven't you looked through the Window to see if Pete is all right? Or just to see him at all? I feel like I don't even know you anymore, Veil. What happened down there that could've changed you so much?"

She studied him, shocked by the question and his concern. It was something she had never experienced, not in her entire existence. Before her journey posing as Veil in

Aureia, she was Lash in Stormcry and she was one of Vulgaar's favourites—the Stormlord had told her as much, but in all the years she had been serving him on Earth and Stormcry he had never asked her if she was all right, or looked at her with concern. Taken aback and not quite sure how to answer, Lash instead reminded herself of why she was in Aureia, this ghastly sunny, warm world, posing as this purple-haired weakling: get close to Shye; hear Sol speak of the Knights; tell Vulgaar what she heard. It wasn't a particularly difficult or intricate plan.

She thought quickly on her feet and pretended to cry. She held her face in her hands and made her shoulders shake with faked sobs, making wailing noises as she advanced on Shye again, who instinctively wrapped her in a hug. He held her awkwardly with his large arms; she felt so small and unfamiliar to him now, yet as she continued to sob uncontrollably, he felt guilty for shouting at her. He gently whispered in her ear, reassuring her that everything was going to be all right. All of a sudden she lifted her face and pressed her lips against his. His eyes flung open in shock and immediately he saw a familiar figure standing in front of them, horrified.

Dusk was watching them. She had seen them kiss. She had seen him open his eyes and now he was looking right at her, the pain and shock clearly visible in her eyes. She stood, shaking for a second or two, then fled as fast as she could. Shye jerked his face away from Veil's and ran after Dusk, keeping focus on her blonde hair flowing behind her. He was faster than her and caught up quickly, grabbing her elbow to spin her around so she was facing him. She was crying quietly, in defeat, refusing to look at him.

"Dusk, please, please believe me. That wasn't what it looked like," Shye implored, trying to initiate eye contact.

She was still looking to the floor, crying. He gently put his fingers under her chin and raised her head so he could see her. It caused him so much pain to see her crying, her bright green eyes dulled by sadness. Dusk's beautiful face was flushed and her cheeks were streaked with tears. She looked up into Shye's eyes, always surprised at how wonderful they were, and she saw in them that he was telling the truth and that he was sorry. She gave him the slightest of smiles. Then she did something she'd always wanted to do. Looking deep into his eyes, she edged forward, wrapped her arms around him, and buried her face in his chest. He was so strong, his arms and chest so firm yet safe and comfortable, and she could feel the chain from his wings pressing against her cheek. She closed her eyes and smiled as she felt him relax and wrap his arms around her too.

At first, Shye didn't know what to do. They'd never been this close before, but as soon as her face pressed against him, he felt as if his heart was going to expand out of his chest and he instinctively hugged her back. He lay his head on hers and gently stroked her hair. It was so soft and silky and ran down her back. He closed his eyes and took a deep breath, inhaling her unique scent and it filled him with comfort. Honey. A gorgeous, sweet, friendly smell and one of the things he loved most about her. Reluctantly he let her go and took a step backward very slowly, then took her hand and gazed into her eyes. She still looked hurt and confused, searching his face for some explanation. He relented and tried to offer her one.

"Dusk, I'm sorry but we can't. You know we can't. You're amazing and I—well, I…" He couldn't finish and looked down at their joined hands. Dusk smiled and squeezed his hand.

"We can, Shye. We can do this. I'd give up my wings,

my life, and even Aureia to be with you. Please?" She began to cry again, trying to swallow the lump in her throat to prevent the tears falling. "Please, can we just— try?" She said the last word in a whisper and gazed deep into his eyes. They were sad and regretful. He raised his hand up and pushed his long hair from his face. It was a little habit of his that she knew so well, a thing he did when he was thinking seriously.

Shye frowned and felt his heart sink, knowing that he couldn't give her the answer she wanted. He raised his grey eyes to meet her green ones, he was hurting deeply and could see she was too. He let go of her hand and turned to leave, trying to hide his tears. Dusk grabbed his arm and spun him around, bringing them together again, forcing him to look at her. He was still trying to turn away, and she cupped his face with her hands, holding him so that he had to look straight into her eyes, into her soul. He was so strong, she could feel his jaw tense under her fingers, his arms and chest growing rigid with anxiety. She knew he wanted to pull away but she wasn't going to let him.

"Shye, you can see how I feel about you. Don't pull away from me. Please talk to me. I love you, Shye. Everything about you, you're strong and brave and kind and protective of all the Guardians in your charge. Now, you talk," she ordered with a satisfied grin on her face, believing she had won.

Shye looked back at her, relishing the sensation of her fingers on his face. He relaxed his muscles so as not to scare her and placed his large hands on her waist, his fingers once again touching that soft hair that he loved so much, flowing down her body. His gaze drifted to her lips. They were red and full and they looked so lovely when she was telling him off. He smiled down at her, a big smile that lit his eyes and she mirrored it. She tilted her head up to his and he bent towards her. They were inches apart, his arms now wrapped around her properly. He felt her sweet breath on his face, and he panicked. He pushed her away, suddenly, and more harshly than he intended.

She stumbled backwards, looking up in horror, so confused. She tried to fight the tears as she watched his shoulders slump. He smiled sadly at her, regret and sympathy in his eyes, and held his hands out in defeat before turning and walking away. This time, Dusk let him go.

Shye wandered around Aureia for an hour or so. He felt crushed. There was nothing he could do to make him or Dusk feel better and he knew it. He found himself at the Window and sat cross-legged, resting his chin on his hands. Looking down at the cities below him, he smiled as he thought of the missions the Guardians had completed over the years; the countless people they had saved. He always took comfort in knowing he belonged to something very good and powerful. At that moment, a burst of sunlight surrounded him, a friendly heat that consumed him completely. He closed his eyes to concentrate on the blissful feeling, knowing at once what it was and becoming even more integrated with that great power. The heat dissipated a little, but there was still warmth covering his back. Shye remained cross-legged, letting his arms rest on his legs, his head raised so he was alert for the message he was about receive. The hot spot on his back was moving slowly and he heard the voice of Sol.

"Don't turn around, young Shye, you shall hurt your eyes." Her voice was elegantly female, yet held a presence of power and knowledge. He grinned; she began the same way each time she appeared to him.

"Why do you not pursue your feelings for Dusk? She cares a great deal for you."

Shye thought of how to answer, however he sensed she might already know the answer. He lowered his head slightly and his chestnut hair flopped forward around his face. He pursed his lips as he considered a response, feeling a sadness grow in the pit of his stomach, welling up into his throat. He swallowed the sob back and then he felt the warmth on his back envelop his whole body—a supportive gesture from Sol that almost felt like a hug. He smiled and raised his head.

"I think you know why," he said speculatively, turning his head slightly and raising one eyebrow in her direction before continuing; "I love her beyond anything I've ever known, Sol. When she's near me I feel—I don't know— sort of as if I am floating free and glued to the spot at the same time. I too would offer my wings and my life and even my home to be with her and keep her safe." He paused to collect his thoughts, knitting his brow as he forced the next words out, truly not wanting to believe them.

"However, if I gave her my wings and she offered me hers, and if I were to die on Earth, in battle, she would die too, right?" he asked. He knew the answer but still sought the confirmation from the Sun Priestess. She was quiet for a few moments and retracted some of her heat from his sitting frame. Shye had never seen Sol; he didn't know if anyone had, but he didn't need to see her. The heat that comforted him was proof enough that she was real.

"Yes, you are correct, young Shye. But you are both very skilled warriors. Why would you assume your fate was to die?"

"I don't assume, Sol, I am just apprehensive. If I were to be killed and dragged Dusk with me, I could never

60

forgive myself. Even if she could and we were together after, I'd always be weighed down with guilt in the knowledge I allowed the other half of my soul to die, because I acknowledged that I love her. It's too selfish of me." He slumped again and put his fingers to his forehead, massaging in a soothing motion, trying to eradicate the feelings he had just exposed. There was no warm hug this time. It was a ball of pure heat moving across his back. He stared down to Earth, for the first time feeling jealous of the ground walkers. They could love freely, the greatest possession any of them have is the ability to love one another in a million different ways. How he envied them as he watched. He was brought out of his reverie by the powerful yet calming voice of the being behind him.

"Do not grow envious, young Shye; our ground-walking friends are not without their troubles or trials. That is why we are here, to guard them, and you and Dusk are both magnificent Guardians. You, in particular, are brave and astute, which is why you have a growing concern for our friend, Veil."

Shye raised his head again. This was what he had been hoping for; information to help Veil.

"Shye, I am afraid that your concerns for Veil are valid and you should focus your observations on her at all costs. She could be dangerous."

"Why? Why is she dangerous?"

"I'm afraid I cannot tell you, Shye. Please just trust me. All is not what it seems. Nor should you think too long on your feelings for Dusk. She will not wait forever. You, my young Shye, are destined for great things and she is a big part of them."

At those last words, the heat dissipated and Shye was alone again, looking down through the Window, and searching, hoping for an answer.

Chapter Ten

When Pete had taken the woman home, he had held her for hours as she cried. To Pete, Veil was a beautiful and mysterious stranger and for reasons unknown to him, he wanted to protect her and look after her. It broke his heart to see her so sad. He tried asking her what was wrong, but all that she offered was seemingly random words between her sobs—'sun', 'necklace', 'Draxyl'. He was beginning to believe that she was either on drugs or suffering delusions. He held her tightly, cradling her as they huddled together on his large blue sofa with its big cushions so comfortable that he had often preferred it to his bed. Veil had eventually stopped crying and initially Pete assumed she had calmed down, but then discovered she had actually fallen asleep in his arms. He watched her sleep for a while, taking the time to examine the bruises on her face, which were gradually disappearing, and some colour had returned to her cheeks, although it may have been because she had cried so much. She seemed so peaceful, and yet, though her eyes were closed she continued to frown slightly and she looked so sad. Pete's arm that her head was resting on began to fall asleep and go tingly. Reluctantly, very slowly and gently, he tried to shift position, until he was on the edge of the sofa and cradling her body in both arms. Instinctively, she rested her head on his firm chest and he felt her hair cascade down his arm. He could smell her again, the lavender scent radiating from her, always comforting him. He only hoped he could do the same for her.

He somewhat awkwardly carried her down the small hallway to his bedroom. He stuck out his foot and gently tapped at the slightly ajar door but as it swung back it struck a framed picture resting against the wall behind it. Pete held his breath, tightly shut his eyes and winced, unconsciously raising his shoulders and bringing Veil's sleeping form with them. He opened one eye and looked down. Veil still slept on. He smiled to himself, proud that he was able to carry such a delicate load without disturbing it. He laid her down on his unmade bed and she immediately turned on her side and curled up. Pete reached around her body to grab the ends of a blanket and cover her. He face seemed to relax and a small smile graced her lips. Beautiful, Pete thought to himself, before lightly stepping backwards and out the door, pulling it closed as he went.

Veil was indeed fast asleep and smiling as she enjoyed a wonderful dream…

They were on a rooftop, just the two of them. The sun was setting low in the sky and everything was bathed in warm rich oranges and pinks, the windows of the other buildings reflecting the sky's colours. There were hundreds of candles glowing around them, creating a warmth and dancing light and shadows. And there were flowers, more flowers than Veil had ever seen, scattered around the edge of the rooftop in vases, glasses, jars—some were just lying on the bricks—and there were petals sprinkled at their feet. Pete was standing in front of her, wearing a tuxedo; he had shaved and his hair was combed neatly. He looked happy and content as he stared back at her. She glanced down and found that she was wearing a beautiful ball gown, silky and gold in colour. She could feel her hair tumbling, smooth and clean, down her back and she knew Pete was appreciating how she looked. He reached for her hand, which she accepted, and then she heard music; a soft jazz and a gentle piano. She loved this music for it was easy to dance to. Pete gently pulled her close, resting one hand on her lower back as the other grasped hers and held it up, like ballroom dancers.

As they began to move to the music, Veil thought this must be Heaven. Nothing on Earth or Aureia could ever have compared to this moment of being in Pete's arms in such a romantic setting. Their feet were moving to the soft music and Pete was twirling her around and around on the rooftop. Her gown flowed and twirled at her ankles whenever he spun her and she smiled up into his face to find that he was smiling down at her, gazing at her as though she were the only other person in the world, and that's how she was feeling at that moment; as if it were just the two of them alone on the planet, enjoying a piece of paradise.

Pete spun her around and then dipped her body downward, supporting her back with his strong hands, she bent her legs to accommodate the angle and stop herself falling. As he held her, the sun completely set and it went dark. She looked up into his face and felt her heart race. Now he looked terrified, his eyes wide and the colour drained completely from his cheeks; he wasn't smiling anymore. Suddenly, a gust of wind whistled around the rooftop, extinguishing every single candle and knocking vases over. Everything went dark and it began to rain; thunder crashed over the heads, and a flash of lightning briefly lit up Pete's face above her.

Veil was frightened, but when she tried to move she felt

rooted, stuck in Pete's arms, fighting to look up as the rain trickled down her face. Then she noticed something above her, in the sky, a gap in the dark clouds and relief flooded through her. It was the Window and someone could see her; a Guardian was looking down on her and soon they would come for her. She glanced at Pete to find he was shaking his head in sympathy. Confused, she looked up at the Window again; suddenly her vision zoomed and magnified like a vacuum; the person looking through the Window was her. She was looking down at herself, but her eyes were red and she was smiling maliciously. Veil continued watching in horror, as the creature lifted a white pointy hand and gave a little wave.

Veil looked for Pete again, but he'd disappeared and she fell to the hard floor of the roof. She stumbled to her feet, surrounded now only by rain and darkness. She was scared and alone, she began to scream.

Pete heard Veil crying out in her sleep and ran to his bedroom. She was thrashing around in his bed and shrieking. He touched her arm to wake her up, but nothing happened. He shook her gently.

"Veil?" he called quietly, then a little more urgently, "Veil! Can you hear me? You're dreaming, Veil, wake up. Wake up, Veil, WAKE UP!"

As the shouted words left his mouth, Veil's eyes opened and she shot up into his arms, sobbing. He held her as tight as he could, hoping to make her feel safe. He held her for a long time, stroking her back and whispering reassuring words in her ear.

A flash of lightning lit up his whole bedroom and hard rain began to lash against the windows. Then thunder roared loud and clear over their heads, Veil looked around, her eyes wide with terror. Another blast of lightning made her jump and instinctively wrap her arms around Pete. He looked down at her; *this brave woman who rescued me from a fire and a group of thugs, and she's afraid of thunderstorms?*

"Hey, it's just rain, nothing to be scared of," he said quietly.

She continued to cry uncontrollably and when another clap of thunder erupted she clung onto Pete's clothes, burying her face in his chest.

"Veil, do you trust me?"

She thought for a moment, feeling the safety of his arms around her and his cheek resting on hers as he whispered assurances in her ear. She nodded against him but still gripped onto him with all her strength. He manoeuvred her gently in his lap so that he could lift her around her back and under her knees; her sobbing had ceased but she was still startled every time there was a flash of lightning. Pete carried her out of the bedroom and down the corridor. When they reached the front door, he carefully lifted his knee to support her and used his free hand to open the door. They were walking across a hallway with other apartment doors around them. Pete opened another door that read, 'Roof Access'. Veil saw this and began to panic again. She hid her face in Pete's shoulder as he walked up the stairs. She began to cry and shout again.

"No, Pete! Please I'm afraid. Put me down, Pete. PUT ME DOWN!" She was struggling against him to get free. But Pete was unyielding and continued up onto the roof. When he opened the door, they were immediately greeted with splashes of the harsh rain, whipping winds and loud thunder. Veil eventually broke free and stood on her feet. She looked around the roof and gasped in shock as she realised that it was the same rooftop from her dream. She squinted against the rain hitting her face and turned to run back down the stairs. but Pete grabbed her arm and turned her to face him. He had surmised that she was afraid of the rain due to the attack taking place during a storm and must therefore be suffering with post traumatic stress, which he wanted to rid her of the only way he knew how; by facing it.

"It's just rain, Veil. It can't hurt you. Watch!" He was speaking loudly and enthusiastically. Veil watched in horror as Pete ran out into the storm in the t-shirt and shorts he'd been sleeping in and began dancing and jumping around. She was fascinated, he wasn't getting hurt; there were no Draxyls appearing. Pete seemed to be having fun. He was laughing and dancing like fool, his hair now stuck to his head and his clothes clinging to his body, outlining his defined chest and arms. Veil smiled at him, reminded of her reasons for flying down in the storm. She loved Pete and right now, she felt like she couldn't love him more if she tried. He came towards her, rain dripping from his hair and the end of his nose. He smiled a huge smile and held out his hand to her. She didn't even think about it and held his hand, allowing herself to be pulled out into the rain.

At first she tensed up, not at all accustomed to the feeling of raindrops on her skin, but then she relaxed a little.

"See?" Pete smiled. "Nothing to worry about."

He took her hand again and began to twirl her around the rooftop as they splashed in the puddles. He fell over and waved his arms in the air to make her laugh. Then he rolled onto his back and let out a small grunt of pain. Veil immediately ran over to him, her long wet hair slicked against her back, the large t-shirt he had given her to wear clinging to her skin. She helped him to his feet. Now they were standing inches apart and he reached up to brush the wet hair from her face. They were both gazing into the other's eyes, taking in their wet features. Pete was out of breath, partially due to the activity, but mostly due to the mysterious, beautiful woman standing in front of him.

"My hero," he whispered breathlessly, his gaze straying to Veil's lips. He couldn't help but bend his head to kiss her. Veil raised her face and closed her eyes as she felt his lips touch hers. They were soft, tender—everything Veil had imagined they would be. He pulled her closer until there was not even a fraction of an inch of space between them, the rain trickling down their faces and their lips as they kissed in the storm.

Chapter Eleven

Kin was in his police uniform walking along a sunny street, his short fluffy brown hair poking out of the sides of his hat. He liked being on Earth as a police officer; people respected him and did as he instructed. He felt a lot more powerful here than he did in Aureia, mainly because he was of some use when walking these streets. People came to him for help and he was bigger and stronger than most men on Earth. But not as strong or as impressive as Shye. Kin had made his peace with his station and could only hope that one day he would astound Sol enough with his bravery and fighting skills that she would assign him his own individual to protect, like Veil had Pete. Kin was short for Kindred and he knew he was somehow different to other Guardians; he just didn't know how, other than that he didn't act well under pressure and was almost always afraid. Except for moments like this.

As he continued to stroll down the sunny street, Kin felt commanding and authoritative. He was in control and he was always assigned to safer parts of the city which he didn't particularly mind, as not many other Guardians were in this area and he was therefore alone and the most powerful person in a ten mile radius. Casually, he walked on, nodding as citizens when they smiled at him respectfully.

Then he heard it.

A man's scream of pain came from an alley not far from Kin's current location and he quickly looked in that direction and then all around him. There were plenty of people busying themselves on this sunny street; he could call out if need be. He hooked his thumbs into his police belt and strolled confidently towards the alley, cloaked in shadow due to the angle of the sun and the towering buildings either side, but the closer he got, the less valiant and more apprehensive he became. He could see vast shapes moving vigorously, shadows within shadows, and once he had stepped into the darkness he could only just about distinguish a man on the floor, being beaten by four other much larger men. His instincts told him to run, but he was the authority here; if he told them to stop then they would stop. He took a step closer and collected all of his courage before putting his hand up and shouting.

"STOP! Stop it right now!"

The four male attackers briefly turned to look at the police officer. They all saw it. He had fear in his eyes. They snickered and continued to beat the man lying on the floor. Kin didn't understand. Previous experience, plus Shye's tales of being on Earth and having the authority usually led to the perpetrators ceasing their activity. He looked at them in confusion and repeated, louder and with a hint of danger.

"I told you to stop! STOP! Leave that man alone! Or I'll…"

"You'll what?" one of them barked, interrupting his threat. "Give us a warning? Arrest us? Piss off, pig!"

That comment raised a round of laughs from the assailant and his comrades, who had now forgotten about their victim on the floor and were advancing on Kin. The man on the floor wasn't moving and Kin panicked; he was alone. His four aggressors now had better light on them, and Kin could see their faces; real unmistakable fear began to pound through every part of his body. The biggest of the four had a mess of blue and black spiky hair, his face covered in silver and gold piercings, and his eyes were black. In fact all of the men's eyes were black and the other three had a very similar appearance; dark hair, dark clothing, and in spite of the bright summer day and the sunshine on the other side of the alley that Kin wished he was standing in right now, these four men perpetuated nothing but darkness and gloom. They were sneering and started walking towards him slowly, menacingly, circling him like predatory cats circling their prey. Kin was spinning to keep them all in his sights and making himself dizzy.

"What do you want? I'm armed," he said, reaching for the gun. He hated guns and this one would only fire blanks, but they didn't know that.

"Oh really?" the closest of the men snarled. "What are you and your toy gun gonna do to us, cloud rider?" He snickered at the last part and the others joined in. Kin gasped. They knew he was a Guardian? And they'd referred to him as 'cloud rider'? No one called them that, except Draxyls, he suddenly realised in panic. They must have been hiding in the darkness of the alley. Four Draxyls against one weak cloud rider.

Kin felt his shoulders slumping in defeat but then something happened. Another emotion took over and he took his police hat off and threw it to one side, surprising himself, then popped the gun out of its little holster and threw that as well, a harsh metal scraping sound echoing around the alley as it hit the pavement and slid to a halt a few feet away. The attacked man focused his attention on the gun, his eyes widened in fear as he quickly scrambled to his feet and ran from the confrontation unfolding in the alley. Kin calmly watched him leave, then turned back to the Draxyls, his pale brown eyes dark with anger and courage. He balled his hands into fists at his sides and prepared himself for attack. They had stopped circling now and there was one either side of him, the others in front and behind him. The Draxyl in front was the smallest and his black eyes shone with menace and insanity. He charged at Kin, who in turn surprised them all by striking a blow underneath his chin and sent the Draxyl flying high into the air and striking a wall at the end of the alley, where he fell into a crumpled heap.

The Draxyl behind him was the biggest and grabbed Kin's arms, pinning them to his sides while the other two took turns punching and kicking him, striking his head and face over and over again until he was spitting blood and his eyes were nearly swollen shut. He could hear his ribs cracking and the larger one holding him gave the others a nod, indicating that they should stop. When they did, Kin used all the strength he had left to keep his head raised and look at them defiantly, although his eyes betrayed him, for they reflected pain and sadness. The large one holding him smelled of smoke and sweat and he began squeezing Kin tight. He couldn't breathe; the arms around him felt like they were forcing his lungs together and crushing the bones in his arms and ribs. He cried out in pain and blood filled his mouth again. He felt his wings dangling by his chest and tried in vain to reach them, but his hands wouldn't lift any higher than his hips. He couldn't fight back and he couldn't escape, but Kin made a decision, and he repeated this decision to himself over and over again.

"I am not dying in this alleyway. I am not dying in this alleyway. I am not dying in this alleyway"

He squeezed his eyes tight shut and thought of Aureia; he thought of his friends, and Sol and Unenda, and the

Knights of the Sun, and he felt a heat begin to rise in him. The Draxyls stared at him, astonishment on their faces as a bright orange light started to glow from within Kin's body, growing brighter and stronger until it enveloped him completely. The Draxyl holding him was struggling to keep his grip, but couldn't and released him completely, howling out in pain.

"He burnt me!" he shrieked, rubbing his arms.

Kin stood surrounded by the light, still in excruciating pain, glaring at the Draxyls, his eyes dark and threatening.

"I think it's time you went home," he told them, his voice low and unwavering. The three smaller ones began to back off but the big guy that had been holding him stood his ground and took a step towards the glowing cloud rider. His voice came out in a harsh whisper filled with dread.

"We are home," he said and laughed hysterically, as did his friends. Kin watched in horror as the four of them stepped into the sunshine, out of the shadows. The Draxyl with all the piercings looked up at the sky appreciatively and smiled at Kin before giving a mocking little wave and running away with his cronies following him.

The glow surrounding Kin vanished in an instant and he fell to his knees on the floor, holding his ribs and coughing. He reached up and grabbed the wings dangling from his neck, holding them so tightly that his hands turned white. He banged them against his chest and a white light filled the alley. When it had dispersed, Kin was gone.

Chapter Twelve

A small group of Guardians, including Shye, were standing by the houses near Unenda. Shye was looking up at the tall enigma and wondering what lay atop the building. No matter how long you stood at the bottom and looked for the top, or how high a Guardian flew, the top could never be found. It stretched on for what must be hundreds of miles, Shye had surmised. He and Dusk hadn't spoken all day; he was missing her. He was sad that he had made her sad and hated leaving things as they were, but feared if he tried to reconcile she would reject him. He was so engrossed in replaying their last conversation that he failed to notice the Guardian crawling through the Window until he howled in pain. He turned in the direction of the horrific noise and he ran over.

Kin was barely conscious, muttering incoherences about Draxyls and saving a man, crawling along the ground, his face distorting in pain with each pull of his arms. Shye was big and strong and picked Kin up, carrying him to the healer's hut, while Kin cried out in pain and embarrassment that he was in such a state as to be unable to walk. He looked up into Shye's face, so sturdy and determined and fearless; his facial expression always exuded the appearance of someone wanting to get the job done, and as Kin was being carried away in agony, he envied him for his strength and resolve. He couldn't help but think that if Shye had found himself in a similar situation on Earth he would've been able to defend himself and beat off the Draxyls with little effort.

Kin felt himself being laid down on a rough wooden bed and then Shye was gone, although he remained in the room. A new face appeared, a friendly female face with wisdom and experience in her eyes. Kin felt better already, for this woman was Lorelei—the healer for all those who dwelled in Aureia. Lorelei gently set to work on Kin's ribs, lifting his robe to inspect the injured area and inwardly wincing at the deep dark bruises emerging there. As Lorelei was working on him, Kin surveyed the hut he was lying in. He could make out candles in corners of the room, really big ones with thick lines of wax dripping down the sides. There were also herbs burning all around the confined space that relaxed him and soothed the stinging in his lungs as he breathed in their strange scent,. He smiled and looked up into Lorelei's face again; he and many others had noticed that she was always smiling, with such a powerful radiance about her that it would've been intimidating if she wasn't so warm and comforting with it.

"Kindred, can you tell me how these injuries happened?" she asked. Her voice was low, melodic and entrancing, but the question quickly brought Kin back to reality and he answered in a frightened whisper.

"Draxyls attacked me. In the daylight. They weren't scared or weak; they were really strong and I did my best to fight them off but there were four of them and I couldn't get away." Kin was becoming agitated and Lorelei laid a gentle hand on his shoulder in reassurance. He was having difficulty breathing as he gasped out the words.

"I'm never going back. Please, Shye, don't make go back there! Please promise me, Shye! I cant go back. I won't!"

Lorelei bent down and gently whispered in his ear to calm him. She stroked his face and kissed his eyelids, and as she did so, his panting ceased and he gently fell asleep. She turned her bright blue eyes on Shye, who was struggling to remain calm and keep the horror from his face. He and Lorelei looked at each other, communicating a sense of dread and confusion.

Shye left the healer's hut and went straight to the Window, hoping for quiet so that Sol might appear to him. He stood, arms folded across his chest, the muscles in his jaw clenched in concentration. This wasn't possible. Draxyls weren't on Earth in the daytime, they just weren't. That was the Guardians' time to be there.

"Watchya doin'?" a voice called from behind him. It sounded like Veil, but harsher. He whirled around to see her tiptoeing towards him, her still damaged and unretracted wings twitching.

"I'm thinking, Veil. I wish to be alone. Thank you," he said as politely as he could muster and then returned his gaze to the Window, hoping that she would go away. Veil had always been someone he could converse with for hours; not anymore. This Veil couldn't hold a decent conversation without putting a twisted spin on it. Shye had no desire to speak to her and willed her to leave him alone with his already troubling thoughts.

"Watchya thinkin' about?" she asked, taking another step closer, walking on her toes, bouncing a little into every step. Maybe if she stayed close to Shye for long enough, she could catch a glimpse of Sol. She couldn't understand why he was spurning her advances. After all she looked like Veil; his friend? She was pretty enough, so what was the problem? She looked Shye up and down possessively, but her meanderings were interrupted when he spoke again.

"Kin was attacked on Earth today. He was doing a routine cop watch in a safe neighbourhood. He's saying…" He looked up at her now to make sure he had her full attention then continued; "He's saying Draxyls attacked him."

He watched Veil's reaction with fascination. She gasped and a look of fear crossed her dishevelled features, but then there was nothing. No emotion, not even surprise. They were staring at each other now, both wondering what the other was thinking. Shye was watching Veil intently and she was almost squaring up to him. Finally she broke the silence.

"And?" she asked. "He's obviously confused, Shye. Draxyls don't fly down there in the sun. It hurts them. Their eyes burn and their skin itches. The whole experience is just very uncomfortable! For them." She added the last part quickly. She had been to Earth just once in her time of being a Draxyl and it was not an experience she wished to repeat or even think about.

Shye continued to watch her in curiosity and expectance, and she felt uneasy under his eyes. Beginning to panic that he was onto her, she took a step back. He took a step forward.

"Is that all you have to say?" he asked coldly. This wasn't right. No matter what trauma she had suffered a few nights ago, her indifference was creating anger in him that he hadn't felt before. It was frightening; he felt powerful and frustrated all at once. He took a bigger step towards her this time, but she stood her ground, glaring at him with her purple eyes that now had more prominent flecks of red and black in them.

"One of your best friends is lying in the healer's hut claiming that Draxyls attacked him," he shouted at her. "Dark, menacing, cowardly night dwellers beat him to a pulp when he was outnumbered four to one! Why don't you care?"

This time she did react and looked at the floor guiltily, and strangely, she wasn't acting. She felt bad for the little cloud rider. He was harmless enough and kind of funny.

"I'm sorry, Shye. I…I don't know what to say."

"Then don't say anything!" he snapped and turned away from her. He was becoming more and more scared by his own behaviour. With her head still down, Veil turned and left, shuffling her feet. When she was a few feet away from Shye, she heard someone whispering in her ear, summoning her. Unconsciously she gave a nod and then ran away so fast it became near impossible to see her.

Once Shye was alone, he internally punished himself for his outburst. This wasn't Veil's fault, as far as he was aware. He stood alone and felt truly alone, although he wasn't lonely; he was comfortable with the solitude. Then he felt it, the warm glow stretching across his back and throughout his body.

"Please do not turn around, young Shye, I fear I shall hurt your sight." Sol's voice.

He smiled at this little ritual. Every time she came he was reminded to stay still. He had questions burning in his chest that he needed to know the answers to and took a deep breath to prepare himself for the answers that may follow before he asked his first question.

"Did you help Kin today?" he asked. The heat became a low hum that moved across his back as if she were contemplating her response.

"Yes," she confirmed in her deep knowledgeable voice.

"Were they Draxyls?" Shye asked. He subconsciously swallowed and held his breath awaiting the answer. There was a long pause before he heard again.

"Yes."

Shye felt his heart begin to beat uncomfortably against his chest and a cold chill filled him. Draxyls were on Earth, right now. That thought terrified him.

"Why did you help Kin?" he asked, ashamed at the feelings of jealousy welling within him. Sol had never helped him in moments of crisis on Earth.

"Because, young Shye, your friend Kindred is very powerful; he just doesn't know it yet. Today could have been much worse had I not intervened. Kindred has a destiny to fulfil, just as you and I do, and the attack today was linked with that destiny. Kin will learn from this and become a marvellous warrior, in time."

Not knowing why, these words angered Shye; everything was about destiny when it came to Sol. It was beginning to bother him. Kin wasn't beaten to a pulp to fulfil his destiny; he was attacked because Draxyls were in a place they shouldn't have been. He turned his head slightly in the direction the glow behind him.

"What if I don't believe in destiny?"

Without a moment's pause she answered, "You do."

"How do you know?" he asked, in a small, childlike voice. He knew his destiny was to be with Dusk; he felt it with every inch of himself.

"I can see your heart, young Shye. It beats like that of a warrior and a soulmate. The other half of your soul is hurting now and she will need comforting."

Shye could almost hear the smile in her voice as she said that last sentence. His thoughts momentarily drifted to Dusk and he felt himself smile too. She had really given him a good telling off. His thoughts quickly came back to the present, to Kin and Veil.

"Why were they there, Sol? Why were the Draxyls on Earth?"

This time there was hesitation before she answered; he felt the heat at his back fade away momentarily, and then come back.

"The balance is shifting, Shye. Vulgaar wants control of my Knights and thinks by infiltrating our home and my Guardians he will succeed in obtaining that power. The Draxyls no longer fear you, me or the Knights. Under Vulgaar's influence and instruction they have become much bolder in their visiting patterns to Earth."

Shye nodded as he processed this information. He had anticipated something like this but it still came as a shock. A thought came to his mind.

"Can he get control of your Knights, Sol?"

"No," she answered. "My Knights have free will, of course but they are loyal to me and Aureia. I am not worried."

Shye nodded again, relieved to hear this news. Although he had never seen the Knights of The Sun, he had always wondered, and Aureia was full of rumours and speculation regarding their size and power. Sol addressed him again, this time the heat filled him from the inside out.

"Please do not wait too long to be with Dusk. To you it may seem bleak or doomed but try for me if you can, to see it as hope."

With that, the heat vanished and Shye was left alone once more, mentally preparing himself for the battle between light and dark, and also the battle in his heart.

A few feet away, hiding behind the corner of a house, Veil's eyes were watching and her ears were listening.

But it was Lash's smile edging the corners of that mouth.

Chapter Thirteen

Veil awoke, feeling comfortable, warm and safe; Pete's arms were around her and they were in his bed. He was snuggled up against her back and had his arms tightly wrapped around her. She smiled to herself. *Perhaps,* she thought, *he is holding on so tight because he is afraid I might disappear.* She could feel his heartbeat and his breath against her neck and sighed deeply in satisfaction. Without moving, she glanced around, at each tall window, the sunshine bursting forth into the bedroom, large pillars of light filtering over their bodies on the bed, which to Veil made this morning all the more special, because it reminded her of home. She smiled as she recalled the events of the night before.

She and Pete were kissing in the rain and clinging to each other tightly, their clothes were soaked through and sticking to their skin. Veil was relishing in all the new feelings. She'd never kissed anyone before and this wasn't just any first kiss; this was the first kiss with her first love—her only love—and in the rain. Pete's lips felt as if they were becoming hotter and hotter with each kiss, yet the heat was infused with the coolness of the rain. It was refreshing and extraordinary to experience the rain in this way, no fear or horror surrounding them; it was just Veil and Pete sharing an incredible moment together. They stopped kissing and separated for a few moments but still held each other; she was breathless and her skin felt as if it were ablaze despite the coolness of the rain hitting her. She dared to look in Pete's eyes and was slightly taken aback by what she found there. Pete was taking in every inch of her, gazing at her face; drops of rain were falling from his short hair and eyelashes, running down his cheeks and under his chin. To Veil he had never looked more beautiful and she found herself drowning in his wonderful deep brown eyes that looked even darker and warmer for the rain and the kisses. As they gazed at each other, Veil saw in him exactly what she had hoped to see: friendship, wonder, desire and love. He reached up and gently brushed her wet hair off her face, his fingers grazing her skin. She shuddered and without a moment's hesitation or thought, she put her hand in Pete's and started dragging him back towards the fire escape and down to his apartment. They stumbled into his bedroom, kissing and hitting the walls as they went, knocking some of the pictures down and laughing. They fell in a tumble onto the bed.

Back in the present, Veil was resting contentedly in Pete's arms and thinking how she wanted stay here forever, with him, but she needed to use the bathroom. Without waking him, she gently moved the arm that was resting on her waist and sat up, feeling the sun on her face. She turned around and spent a moment watching Pete sleeping; he looked so peaceful. His breathing was low and steady, his arms were wrapped around his pillow and his feet were dangling out of the covers. She looked out at the sunshine again, closing her eyes so she could feel its warmth kiss her eyelids. Quietly, she pushed herself into a standing position and tiptoed through the apartment to the bathroom, the hardwood floor cold under her toes, except for the patches of sunlight she stepped into. In the bathroom, she took a look at herself in the mirror; she looked so different. The bruises on her face were all but gone, her hair was vibrant purple and shiny like dark glass, her skin was glowing, but it was a new glow and her eyes appeared bright purple, vivacious and twinkling. All in all her appearance struck her to be that of someone in love and very much enjoying being alive, and right at that moment, that described her perfectly.

Veil slowly crooked her neck and pulled her hair to one side in order to look at the skin-branded wings on her back, gradually turning and noticing that much more of the right wing was missing. It no longer covered half the expanse of her back, and the entire bottom section of the wing was missing. She looked suspiciously at the bare skin that should be tattooed with at least five thousand feathers. She frowned, covered herself back up with her borrowed shirt, and used Pete's toothbrush that was standing alone in a cup by his small white sink, preparing to give Pete a minty fresh morning kiss. As she made her way back to the bedroom, the sunlight vanished. Pete's apartment was suddenly dark, full of shadows and very cold. As Veil walked, she felt the hairs on her neck stand up. She felt alone yet at the same time like she was being watched. With this new feeling of dread, she continued with caution towards the bedroom, slowing her steps down and creeping silently, for fear that someone or something may hear her.

Pete's bedroom door was slightly ajar and Veil could see there was light sneaking through the small opening; it wasn't sunlight, however. It was a cool light, like the one you might find when you open your fridge. As she reached his door, she took a deep breath and stood, listening intently with her head slightly cocked to one side. She heard nothing, not even the sound of Pete breathing or snoring. She looked at the door again, wishing it was transparent in order to make sure its remaining occupant was safe and well, but it wasn't, and she placed the tips of her long elegant fingers to the wood of the door to gently push it open. It moved incredibly slowly and made a long leisurely creaking sound, until it tapped the bedside table and came to a stop.

Veil stood motionless, her hand still holding the door open, her arm outstretched and the rest of her body in the doorway. Trying her best to breathe quietly so as not to disturb the possible intruder, she stepped over the threshold and hesitantly scanned the room, seeing only shades of grey filling the space that just moments ago was bursting with morning sunlight. She crept further into the room, looking around her in confusion. Everything appeared the same; the bed was still in the same disarray and Pete's wet clothes were still on the floor; his glass of water still stood half empty on the nightstand. Looking at the glass more closely, she could see that the water appeared to be...moving? The movement was almost undetectable, just a gently swaying back and forth within the confinements of the glass, never spilling out. She sensed movement just outside the large windows and turned her attention to the bustling and what sounded like whispering voices, thousands of voices whispering at once. Veil covered her ears to try and block them out, but as she moved towards the window, the whispers became quieter. She glanced out and down to the street below. It was quite busy, with many people walking in different directions, smiles on their faces. A young mother was pushing her baby in a pushchair, a couple were holding hands and saying sweet things in each other's ears, an elderly gentleman was cautiously looking both ways as he was crossing the street with a cane in his left hand and a red rose in his right.

She leaned her head against the glass as she continued to regard the crowd below her, a gentle smile on her face as she observed these people, content and happy, enjoying their dreary day. Then suddenly, everyone stopped walking, some in mid-step, creating what appeared like a small village of statues. Veil watched intently, her mind filling with confusion, as all of the people slowly began to turn their heads in her direction, then with one swift motion, every single person she could see were now staring right at her, including the baby sat in his pram. And they were no longer smiling; all the expression had left their faces and a blackness had consumed their eyes—total blackness. As she watched, their skin grew pale and cracked in places. The elderly gentleman who had been carrying the red rose was now holding just a stem, black petals on the ground around his feet. His dark staring eyes and pasty skin made him look tremendously sinister and for unknown reasons Veil feared him the most.

There was a crash from above her, an almighty clap of thunder and the room illuminated with a flash of lightning that momentarily highlighted every surface and angle as it struck the street outside in an explosion of cold light. Veil slowly turned her face upward and what she saw made her legs weak beneath her and beads of sweat formed on her forehead and above her top lip. The crowd began to move as one unit, every step was in sync with the other as they began to slowly make their way to the window through which Veil was watching this terrifying scene unfold. She tried to back away, only to find her feet heavy and stubbornly refusing to move. The dark clouds that had magically appeared above her head cracked open and rain began to pour down in Pete's bedroom, making her clothes wet again. It kept coming down harder and harder, the room now a shallow pool, soaking Veil up to her ankles.

Desperately, she looked down at the rise of water, the room filling with shadows as the Draxyls made their way through the windows and into Pete's bedroom.

Panic was now occupying all of her senses. Veil was trapped and a hundred Draxyls were trying to smash through the windows in order to reach her. Once they had she knew there would be no fight or escape, only death. This realisation gave her a rush of adrenaline, and it was a terrible rush. She was full of fear and dread and a strange energy that she couldn't do anything with. She was still trapped, wet and feeling the horror of the situation crash around her. The old man with the rose was manically clawing at the air with long, dirty nails, his face twisted with an almost demonic aggression, his mouth dripping with what could have been venom with the ferocity of his attack. As she continued to back away from the mob consuming the moderate bedroom, her back hit a wall and the fear coursing through her body caused her to crumple to the floor. She looked up into the faces filled with hatred and evil, trying to shield her eyes so as not to see their animalistic behaviour, but she could still hear their screams of terror, hear their teeth gnashing together, feel their hot rancid breath mingling into one horrifying gust of air propelled by their exertion, their venomous spit and intentions being rained upon her. But the most petrifying aspect of this relentless attack was that Veil could feel their hatred, violence and disregard for life seeping into her mind, their screams penetrating her heart and thus it began to falter under the weight of their persistent savagery. Veil, like every other Guardian in existence, could feel a light within, a warmth providing strength and love for all those around them. In this instance however, Veil could literally feel that same light being extinguished, the breaths of these Draxyls were blowing away her spirit, as if she were a dwindling flame surviving in the shadows and the wind. The thought filled her with dread and she began to sob, her arms wrapped around her legs, her tears falling so quickly she could feel them rolling down her arms and legs and see them landing on the floor and forming puddles as they mingled with the water falling from the ceiling clouds.

The feeling of utter despair consumed Veil, reducing her to a quivering wreck. On Earth, as Pete's lover she was vulnerable, intimidated and fearful. Not long ago she had fought four Draxyls alone to ensure Pete's safety and now here she was cowering in the corner, hoping for someone to rescue her, that Pete would be her saviour. But as she looked again into the fierce mangled faces above her, taunting and cruel, there was no Pete, or friend, or Sol—a realisation that made her sob harder as she watched her attackers through fearful, watery eyes.

Abruptly, the brutal and savage noises desisted. Though it continued to rain onto their faces, they were suddenly still and silent. Veil squinted through the internal downpour at the statues facing her now, their faces completely void of emotion. The happy people she had observed through Pete's bedroom window, pleasantly strolling along a sunny Seattle street, smiling and greeting one another, were gone now. Facing her in this moment, were soulless entities, no spirit or life force. All she saw was blank expressions and pitch-black eyes, glaring at her through the rain and somehow more unnerving than the howling and scratching. The old man with the rose stem and cane was drawing her attention, his thinning grey hair flattened to his head, a few strands slicked down on his cheeks; Veil watched as his thin grey lips began to twitch and, unlike the others in the room, his eyes blinked a few times. He placed his cane on the floor to steady himself, as

91

he leaned shakily towards her. She instinctively drew her knees closer to her body and covered her face with her arms by way of protection. His lips were now a few inches from her ear, and all she could hear for a short moment was the rain falling and his cold breath, the short rasps against her skin making it prickle and crawl with fear. She heard him lick his lips as he prepared to speak and glimpsed his hand over the head of his cane; it was colourless and bony. Drawing in a breath, Old Man spoke into her ear, his voice a low, thin hiss.

"We've won."

Veil's head snapped up and she looked right into the eyes of Old Man, black and hollow, but in them she saw him. She felt him. Vulgaar. He had won a battle that had commenced as she was enjoying a warm bed and the body of her beloved. Old Man was almost nose to nose with her now, smirking in arrogance and victory, and Veil matched it, a spark of vitality and purpose shining through her own purple orbs. The rain was streaming down their faces and she blinked to shed the drops from her eyelids, acknowledging that she was now addressing a very powerful being, no longer a mere Draxyl posing as an old man, but Vulgaar himself. Their breath mixed now they were so close. Still looking into his eyes, Veil replied in a strong, defiant whisper.

"We've not yet begun."

He withdrew abruptly. She continued to smirk, even more so at the expression of surprise on his face. He looked to his minions behind him, still expressionless, staring ahead at nothing, then back at Veil, the rain still pouring. She was vulnerable and strong simultaneously, still with her knees and arms protecting her small frame, but her face exuded conviction and fortitude. It struck him, almost physically, that he didn't frighten this young cloud rider.

But no matter; she was on Earth and her double in Aureia. With this renewed thought, his smile returned and he leaned towards her again, reached out his hand, bringing up his index finger with its sharp pointed nail, and with a catlike motion scratched her cheek.

Veil gasped loudly and sprung up in bed, covered in sweat and panting heavily. She surveyed her surroundings: she was in Pete's bed and he was next to her, the sun was streaming in through his large windows and wide strips of light trailed across their legs. There was no rain, no thunder—just the warmth and the comfort of Pete's presence and his bed. Veil sat back against the headboard and touched her cheek. As soon as her fingers grazed the area, a sharp sting shot through the right side of her face and she grimaced in pain. Pete stirred and looked up at her, smiling at first, then in shock. He sat upright and examined the deep scratch on Veil's face; she was dripping wet, shaking and looked utterly petrified.

"Veil? What's happened?"

He waited but she didn't answer, her eyes were darting around searching for something, though he didn't know what and he intimated that she didn't either.

"Veil? Talk to me, please! What happened to your face? Veil, what's happened? What's going on? VEIL!"

She looked at him now, and what he saw rocked him to the core. She was terrified, perhaps in shock, given that she couldn't stop shaking. She continued to look at him, though not in the eye, struggling to catch her breath. She lowered her eyes for a second and then raised them again to meet Pete's.

"I need to go home."

Chapter Fourteen

Vulgaar stood, waiting patiently, his arms folded across his chest. He looked confident and yet impatient; he was the boss and the boss didn't agree with being made to wait. Three days he had been waiting for the information he so desperately sought. Three days his most trusted and impressively vicious Draxyl, Lash, had been playing the role of that purple cloud rider and three days on he was still no closer to obtaining the Knights of the Sun. If he were to have this redoubtable power, the Knights fighting for his cause, then Stormcry and all those who dwell within it would be unstoppable. He frowned and ran his fingers down the bridge of his nose; frustration was a petty emotion, one he was unfortunately very much accustomed to. His thoughts turned to Sol. Her order in Aureia was sickeningly powerful, and to say that he was envious would be an immense understatement. Envy was a luxurious feeling that he had conquered many years ago. No, what Vulgaar felt for Sol and her kingdom was nothing short of anguished need.

His Draxyls had the ability to reign terror during the hours of night, cloaked and hidden in order to release their pent-up violence and frustration amidst the animals known as humanity. But Vulgaar wished for more; he wanted days too—all the hours, minutes, seconds, breaths, cries and screams that could be drawn out and consumed by his henchmen. The mere thought of this gave him a pleasant shiver all the way through his cold, skinny form. It was an enticing thought; power over Sol, power over humanity, full control of the Knights, a prospect he basked in on a daily basis. The cloud riders and their warrior façade—they wouldn't last a minute against his vast force, he knew it, they knew it and Sol knew it. That's why she'd proposed this ridiculous division of allocated time on Earth between her subjects and his; to avoid conflict. But Vulgaar and his Draxyls thrived on conflict, on savagery and war. That pitiful Guardian, Veil, didn't know what she was talking about in that dream, her confidence was naïve and wrongly placed. How simple it was to take her wings and replace her in Aureia! The foolish girl was beaten to a pulp before she had time to notice it was raining. Vulgaar smiled at this memory, recalling how easy it had been to keep her on Earth, and soon the final battle would be fought. He would have the Knights of the Sun fighting in his corner, for days, weeks, months on end if needs be, until the Guardians had been swatted from the universe, like flies from a picnic, and then the days and nights would be open to his command and terror.

Just one hitch had occurred thus far in his plan: Lash had yet to provide the vital information he needed. Surely it could not take this long to obtain a little information from the cloud riders? He knew of Shye and admired his spirit as that of a warrior, but otherwise he should have cracked within hours of Lash appearing as his friend. Now Vulgaar needed her to return with the news he desperately wanted to hear. Turning slightly away from the vision of Earth below him, he heard her soft footfall come alongside him. He turned towards the noise and saw his loyal spy, Lash, still in her cloud rider costume.

She had deteriorated and her wings were missing several feathers, twitching with each step. He knew of Veil, and that she was beautiful, famed for her head of wonderful, healthy purple hair, but this portrayal of her had stringy, greasy hair with only the slightest tint of colour. Her skin was dull, her smile false and harsh. He looked her up and down, taking in the sickly sight before him.

"Take that off!" he ordered.

"But why? Is this not what you wanted? Look, Master…" She reached up and gently ran her fingers over the pendant hanging from her neck. "I have wings." Lash released a terrifying cackle, an insane noise that disturbed even Vulgaar.

"Take it off, NOW!" he bellowed, pointing with his bony finger. His voice carried a horrific volume and tone, so much so that Lash jumped back and nodded slowly. Once again she reached up for the pendant, only this time her hand was shaking. Her hands went around to the back of her neck to unclasp the necklace, and as it fell to the floor, the purple in her hair seemed to drain away, leaving behind her own deep red hair with the black tips. Her skin turned pale and the plain grey robe disintegrated, leaving behind a black outfit, torn and loosely fitted. Finally, Lash closed her purple eyes and reopened them to reveal the colour of dirty silver, looking Vulgaar squarely in his own red tormenting eyes.

Still keeping her eyes on those watching her, she tucked the pendant into her trouser pocket, defiantly raised her chin and awaited her impending reward for successfully infiltrating the realm of Aureia. Vulgaar approached her. In just a few quick strides he was inches from her face, his tight lips drawn back, exposing sharp teeth.

"Do you have anything to tell me?" he asked in a quiet, intimidating voice.

Lash stepped back, putting a foot of distance between them, staying on the balls of her feet in case she needed to make a quick escape from the fury that she had come accustomed to from her master. She kept a straight and determined look upon her face.

"Any moment now, Vulgaar. The cloud riders trust me. They suspect nothing and soon enough I shall have the secret of the Knights to share with you."

Vulgaar stared unblinking, almost statue-like, harsh breaths being expelled through his nose, effectively penetrating her unyielding barrier with his eyes, then shifting his gaze, his red eyes raking over her body in a most menacing manner.

"But I know that Sol controls them!" Lash added quickly.

Vulgaar smiled—a brief short smile that held only pity and contempt.

"We know Sol controls them, you fool! What we don't know is how. How does she control them?" He had turned his back on her now, rubbing his temples with his cold fingers. Still with his back to her, he dropped his hands and grinned tightly. Slowly he turned to see Lash looking to the ground and trembling. He took a few steps towards her again, slow and predatory, his eyes taking in her cowardly posture, and he laughed quietly as he put himself in her personal space, nothing between them now. Lash squeezed her eyes shut as his breath invaded her senses, his presence so close that her stomach lurched in fear. She prayed, however irrational, that by keeping her eyes closed she would magically cause him to vanish, but she knew that was impossible. Her fear doubled as she felt his long bone-like fingers grasp her chin and pull her face up to meet his. Her breath came out as a whoosh through her nose and her eyes remained squeezed shut, trying hard to banish this reality from her vision. She started to imagine herself back in Aureia. It was warm there, she felt cared for…

SMACK!

Lash's face was thrown to the right as the back of Vulgaar's hand solidly connected with her left cheek. She kept her eyes tight shut, refusing to cry out or display any pain. The left side of her face stung, it felt hot and swollen but still she remained quiet and unmoving. Vulgaar's eyes roamed her face, trying hard to penetrate the resilient exterior, but to no avail. Her eyes remained shut, her face unwavering. Now she felt his fingers gently stroking where he had just struck her, soothing the swelling with the coldness of his hand. It was comforting and eased her pain, but still his touch lacked warmth, concern and love. His fingers emanated control and degradation, even with their featherlight touch against her stinging face. There was nothing but malicious intent beneath them. After a few moments she opened her eyes and looked upon his face. It was calmer now and his eyes were alight with a new purpose, a new idea. He grinned, swallowed and then spoke in a voice that was low and filled with determination.

"Go back there. Figure out what they are hiding and then come back here and tell me. No excuses, no more chances and no more denying who you really are, Lash. You are a Draxyl, my most powerful weapon, and you will do as I ask." He paused, took a long, cleansing breath and continued. "Shye must have something important to him? Something worth bargaining with? Think now." As he finished speaking, his fingers left her face but his eyes stayed glued to her, gauging her reaction.

She was thinking, mentally scanning the crowd of Guardians with whom Shye was acquainted, people he surrounded himself with, those he spoke about. A spark of recognition flashed across her features, causing Vulgaar to smile in victory.

"There is someone?" he enquired.

Lash didn't speak right away. She tried to clear her face of any indication that she had made this mental discovery, but it was too late. She knew that lying now would be futile. She simply nodded and looked into his face awaiting her next command, knowing that after her time in Aureia, her loyalty no longer lay with the dangerous figure in front of her, but with those she was ordered to betray.

Chapter Fifteen

Shye was at the Window; his hair was loosely tied behind his head with a few strands tickling his cheeks. He couldn't see Veil or Pete; there was a fog surrounding the area of Seattle he was searching, a dense unmoving fog that his Guardian eyes could not penetrate. His mind was full of questions and they all centred on Veil's return. Nothing about her reappearance was sitting comfortably with him. His thoughts strayed to Dusk, and he wondered if she had the same reservations he did about Veil. They were often on the same level of thinking when it came to issues in Aureia; she was as fiercely loyal as he was; that was one of the things he loved most about her.

He felt her presence before he saw her. She was standing next him, her very long hair being moved by the gentle breeze and Shye felt it on his arms, a pleasant tingling sensation left in its wake. He turned to face her and was immediately struck by her expression. Her green eyes appeared weary and apprehensive as she looked down through the Window. Neither spoke, but Shye was always happy to be in silence with Dusk, to just simply be. After a few moments however, Dusk broke the silence.

"You're here again?" she asked.

Shye took a deep breath and tried to calm his heartbeat, which always increased when she was present.

"There is a barrier of some description around the area

where Veil was attacked. Don't you find it strange that she hasn't been back here to watch Pete? Before her assault, we couldn't get her away."

"You're right, Shye. I do find it odd. I find her behaviour peculiar also. She seems so, I don't know, twitchy and sarcastic? She's even come across a little mean to a few of the Guardians. I don't think her traumatic event would be enough to warrant such behaviour, not from a Guardian who was once admired by all of her peers. She doesn't seem concerned or protective of anyone anymore."

Shye nodded as she voiced her observations, relieved he wasn't alone in his suspicions. He felt her fingers brush against his, causing the familiar warmth to travel from his hand and up his arm. He smiled and laced his fingers with hers, grateful for the support from her, regardless of their quarrel the previous day. They stepped back slightly from the Window as Shye was trying to decide whether to tell her about his conversation with Sol. He looked into her eyes, so beautiful and vibrant, becoming lost for a few moments as he watched those eyes scan his whole face and then rest on his own, a look of anticipation within them. He had to break the connection; it was becoming too intense and he looked down at their feet as he spoke.

"I'm worried for Veil too. Her whole demeanour seems so unsettled and even her movements strike me as unnatural, like she's stumbling around lost in a world she's known forever. I worry that her encounter has left her unbalanced and a danger to herself." He saw Dusk nod in agreement and she gently squeezed his hand.

"There's been talk, Shye. All the Guardians are scared after Kin's attack. They fear going to Earth, afraid of Draxyls hurting them during the day. Is it true that's become a possibility? That our worlds are leaking into one

102

another? If that is true, what could have happened to make this possible? Do you think Veil knows about it?"

Shye's brows drew tightly. "I have no idea, Dusk. I had not considered the two matters to be connected in any way. I just know that Veil is not acting like herself and fear for people and Guardians alike on Earth during day or night, knowing that Draxyls are down there with the power and violence they can harness. It is an incredibly dangerous place to be."

He briefly turned his face towards the Window, feeling powerless that there wasn't more he could do, that he was unable to solve the problems plaguing his home and his family. Dusk softly tugged on his hands to regain his attention. His troubled eyes returned to her face and he offered a small smile, both in reassurance and because he always felt a little better in the company of Dusk. She was friendly, objective and extraordinarily kind and although his intense feelings for her often impaired his convictions, sometimes resulting in arguments, it was becoming increasingly difficult to resist the power she held over him. Dusk tugged his hands harder now, to stop him daydreaming as she spoke with some urgency.

"We need to figure this out, Shye. Think. Is there anything you know that could help us? Something Sol has told you? You're the only one that she speaks to."

Shye thought frantically. Was Dusk onto something?

"I tell you everything, Dusk. There is nothing I know that you don't." He explained as if it was a common fact; that she did know all that he did.

"NO!" she shouted and dropped his hands. "There has to be something. Something about…the Knights perhaps? Has Sol told you anything about them?" She pushed her face closer, her eyes burning into him.

Again he shook his head.

"All I know about the Knights of the Sun I have told you." He began to look at her suspiciously. Why ask him these questions? She already knew all the answers.

She closed her eyes, releasing her hold on his hands as she took a few steps back. When she opened her eyes again, they were glassy with unshed tears, pleading with him, begging him silently to give her the right answer. Then she spoke again, in a voice that didn't sound like it belonged to her, defeated and weak.

"Please, Shye. Just tell me about the Knights. We need to figure out how to harness their power, just tell me? Please?"

Shye stared at her, bewildered by both her behaviour and her questions. He held his hands up, his palms facing her, indicating a surrender and that he had nothing further to offer. Taking a step towards her he spoke low and gently.

"Dusk, why are you asking me these things? I've already told you. You know what I know. I have no further information, only what Sol has divulged to me. Please tell me what's wrong."

Dusk turned her back to him, wiping the tears from her face. Her arms fell to her sides and she squared her shoulders before speaking again. Now her voice held confidence and purpose.

"I didn't want to do this, but you've left me no choice."

She began to tremble slightly, then more violently and so quickly that Shye could not see any distinguishing movement. For a few moments she was just a blur and when she had stilled, Dusk's long flowing blonde hair was replaced with purple unhealthy thin strands, her back had wings that were jerking slightly and her feathers looked dull, many of them missing. As she turned slowly her face was now Veil's, but pale and tired, her eyes black and hollow, like there was no one behind them, no soul. She tilted her head to the side, examining him. She felt uncomfortable scaring him, and did not like his reaction to her appearance at all, but she had orders to follow. She fluttered the wings behind her, making a few more feathers fall, and then sauntered towards him, bearing her teeth, pointy and like shiny metal. She spoke menacingly her voice rasping.

"Last chance. Tell me how to harness their power, how to control them, right now, or else."

Shye was frozen in shock. Why would Veil want to know? She looked terrible. He took a step back, afraid of her actions. But in his muddled state he could only think of one thing to ask, and as soon as he voiced it, realised it was the wrong thing to say.

"Or else what?"

She grinned and indicated her head to the left, to the space above the Window. When Shye mimicked the move, Dusk appeared in a flash. She was levitating over the space, frantically reaching to her chest for her wings but her pendant wasn't there. She looked to Shye and tried to call out to him for help but when she opened her mouth, no sound was forthcoming. Shye looked back to Veil.

"What are you doing? Veil, let her go!" The panic was rising through him now. He couldn't let anything happen to Dusk, he couldn't.

Veil looked down through the Window now, towards Earth and nodded her head indicating to Shye to do the same. Trying to keep his defensive stance, he gently leaned his head and cast his eyes downward. His hands fell in front of him, his eyes widened and his heart momentarily stopped. An overwhelming terror swept through his entire body, leaving him feeling cold and yet hot at the same time.

Below where Dusk was being invisibly imprisoned, there was no longer Earth—no buildings, grass, fields, streets, people or sunlight. The entire area as far as he could see was dark and heaving with the bodies of Draxyls; millions of them, eyes black and staring, their sharp teeth bared, animalistic, and as they screamed and spat, venom spewed from their lips. They were snarling, biting, clawing at the air, at each other, and all the while looking up through the Window, millions of black, soulless eyes watching, their attention centred solely on Dusk, waiting for her to be dropped into their mass like live bait.

Shye was in a state of hysteria and wanted nothing more than to run at Veil and force her to release Dusk, but he maintained an exterior of calm and control. His eyes shifted from below them, up to Dusk and then back to Veil, trying to exhibit an air of indifference even though knew his eyes were betraying him. He looked at Veil threateningly.

"Let her go," he commanded in a low, menacing voice.

Veil, who was becoming more dishevelled with each passing second, put her index finger to her chin in false contemplation and cast her eyes upward. When they landed back on Shye he felt as if he was about to stumble backward, but held strong, staring into her eyes. They were silver and reflective, making it impossible to gauge her reaction or know if she were being deceitful.

"Can't do it, Shye, not until you give me what I need. And if you don't? Well then…"

She quickly snapped her head in Dusk's direction and she dropped a few feet into the space of the Window.

"NO!" Shye screamed reaching out to her. She stopped falling again, but was still suspended over the beasts below. He turned back to Veil to find her watching the scene unfold with a smirk on her face. He took a step forward.

"What do you want, Veil?" he asked, sounding more confident than he felt.

She peered at him, eyes narrowed and lips twisting.

"Look into my eyes, cloud rider. Veil isn't home."

She said it so cruelly that Shye was stunned that the words were coming from Veil's lips. Was she saying she wasn't Veil? He frowned, confused; this whole scenario was so strange to him. She spoke again, regaining his full attention.

"Now. I hate to press you," she said so sweetly, "but I need some information. How does Sol access the power for the Knights of the Sun?"

Shye was really lost now. Why would she need to know that? If he told the truth, he put Dusk's life on the line but if he lied she may sense it.

"Sol has told me that she doesn't hold the power of the Knights. They are loyal to her of their own free will. That is all I know, I swear it. Now please let her go."

He decided to go with the truth, knowing that the information probably wouldn't help her anyway. Shye was beginning to feel the pieces fall into place, his memory scanning the events of the last few days. Veil's tumultuous return, her erratic behaviour, the questions, Kin's attack; it was all somehow making sense and yet not entirely. There was just one question at the forefront of his mind right now.

"Where is Veil?"

The person looking at him chuckled ruefully but didn't answer. Her silver eyes held a secret and her wings twitched painfully. Shye looked to Dusk. She was terrified and begging with her eyes for his help. He would not lose Dusk; nothing was worth that much. He could feel his heart breaking and soul screaming with each passing second that she was in danger. He turned his attention back to the person in front of him.

"Where is Veil? And who the hell are you?" He was taking small steps towards her now and she was standing her ground, but he saw a flicker of something cross her features. Fear? Regret? Sadness?

She didn't answer him straight away, she shook her head as if to clear her thoughts and then said, "Say bye bye, Dusk."

Shye watched in horror as Dusk's eyes filled with panic and then she dropped with no warning, towards the Draxyls below.

"NOOOOOOOOO!" Shye screamed and ran towards the Window, putting his hands to his chest to fly down and save her, but as he reached up a pain ripped through his entire body. He collapsed to the floor, trying to breathe, but no air would enter his lungs. The creature wearing Veil's face sauntered towards him and bent down. She watched him writhing around, both from the pain she was inflicting using her mind and the heartache that must be splitting him in half. She reached out and stroked his cheek. He grimaced; her fingers were rough and cold. He squeezed his eyes against the pain and felt the tears running down his face. Dusk was gone. She was gone and he didn't stop it.

"I told you I didn't want to do this, Shye. I tried everything else I could think of. Now you are going to tell me what I want to know or I'm going to…"

But her words died on her lips as a staggering orange glow appeared behind her. Shye's pain diminished as he squinted against the light, so unbelievably bright. He raised his hand to his face to block it and could see vague shapes of animals, men and weapons but nothing clear enough for him to make out. A tear fell from Veil's eye and she began to shake. The heat was everywhere. She was hot and the ends of her wings were singeing in the glow. It became hotter, the light so bright that Shye had to turn his face away to try and guard himself from it. Then he heard it: a voice. A voice that was deep and commanding; a voice of more than authority, almost divine in its intensity.

"Stand," the voice commanded.

Veil did so, with her back to the bright glow, the heat on her back and wings. She was shaking more violently now, for she knew who was behind her. She could feel them. She could hear the footfall of the animals they rode and the metal of their swords against shields. She listened and heard the voice again, rich and low.

"Neither our world nor our dreams are for your invasion. Go back to who sent you. Tell him we are a loyal fellowship and not to be bargained for. You will not return."

Veil simply nodded and looked down at Shye, his head still turned away from the light to protect his eyes. She let a few tears roll down her cheeks and whispered, "I'm sorry."

With a small blast of light she vanished. The glow was slowly fading, the heat on Shye's body declining, and he raised his head quickly to catch a glimpse of who had been there, but there was nothing; just empty space. He quickly crawled to the Window to see if Dusk was there. Once again there was just empty space, a dark nothingness that he felt himself falling...falling...

Shye awoke with a start. He was sweating and in his bed, in Aureia. He held his hand to his heart to feel it thumping furiously in his chest and tried to calm it as his surroundings came into focus. It was a dream; the whole ordeal was a dream. He smiled at this revelation, not worrying about what it meant for Aureia. In that moment he didn't care where Veil was or who was in her place. All he wanted to do was see Dusk. She was alive and they would be together. He jumped from his bed and ran to find her. He needed to find her and tell her that he couldn't imagine a life with her missing from it. She had through all of these years become a part of him—quite possibly the best part of him.

He strode towards the place Dusk slept, renewed with what he considered his greatest purpose, and as he drew closer he quickened his pace, almost running now, prepared to unmask himself and show her that he felt the same way she did; he always had. He would not spend another second without her, and he was going to tell her right now.

He reached her hut and found her asleep on her back on her small cot, her long hair splayed across her pillow, glowing in the kisses of the eternal sunshine pouring through her window. He stood and watched her for a few moments as her chest gently rose and fell with even steady breaths, for a few moments content to watch her being here, alive and not in fatal danger. But he was bursting to talk to her. He kneeled next to her bed and gently shook her shoulder, whispering her name. Her bright green eyes blinked open slowly and focused on him next to her bed, making her smile immediately.

"Shye?" she spoke in a rough, sleepy voice. "What are you doing here?"

He just gazed at her. All of the inspired, extravagant thoughts of love and forever that had been in his mind since he woke up and now, facing the other half of his soul, he couldn't think of what to say. He swallowed and swallowed again before speaking.

"Dusk, I'm sorry. I am so sorry I have been such a fool. Trying in vain to pretend that I don't love you, to push you away and make you stop trying. But the truth is, Dusk, that what I feel for you is beyond love, it's greater and deeper than love. Because you're my better half and…"

Shye paused, unsure of how to continue. He looked up at her and saw that she was crying. He reached out and wiped a tear from her cheek, marvelling at the softness he found there.

"I know that there are risks involved. I know that we will at times perhaps regret this decision. But I also know I don't care anymore. I belong with you forever and you with me. I want to give you my wings, Dusk. I think they should be with you always."

He raised his hand to her chest and laid his palm flat against her heartbeat, coming strong and fast below his warm fingers.

"Right here, next to your heart, so I will be there, forever or as long as I can. Dusk, will you join with me? And give me your wings in return?"

Shye took a steadying breath. He had said it. He had told her, finally. Now he looked at her, awaiting an answer.

Dusk was still crying, but smiling fully through her tears. She laid her hand atop Shye's on her chest and moved forward so that her face was inches from his and placed her hand above his heart, feeling strength and softness from him. She swallowed and then whispered.

"Yes."

Chapter Sixteen

Pete stirred the tea he had made for them and placed the spoon on the small dish beside the teapot. Turning to his modest kitchen table where Veil sat, he put her cup in front of her and smiled, but she did not smile back. He sat opposite and watched as she clasped her fingers around the mug to warm them. She hadn't spoken since awakening from her nightmare; the silence and stillness were unnerving him, totally unlike the vibrant and inquisitive woman who had shared his bed for the past few days. She remained quiet, concentrating on the liquid in the cup.

"Wanna tell me what the dream was about?" he asked quietly, not looking at her.

Veil took a long, deep breath, and came forward so that her elbows were resting on the table surface. The cup slid across the table and her chin came to rest on her hands, but her eyes didn't meet Pete's. Instead she fixed her gaze on a mark in the wood in front of her. Where to begin? She thought to herself.

"Pete…" She paused and looked around the kitchen quickly, as if trying to visualise and gather the courage to tell him more of her story. When she looked up, she expected to find impatience or frustration but saw only compassion and serenity in the kind eyes of the man she loved. She loved Pete, he loved her; it would all fall into place, somehow.

"My...family live far from here. It is almost impossible to reach them—almost. To get home, to see my family, would be extremely dangerous, but I have to try. And I have to try soon."

Pete nodded slowly, gently smiling in what he hoped looked like understanding, even though he didn't think Veil was actually making any sense. He thought carefully about his next words before he spoke them.

"I will be more than happy to help you find your family, Veil, but may I ask? Why the urgency? Does it have something to do with the dream you had?"

"The urgency is that I know my family are in danger. I feel it. I feel them. A great threat is about to befall them and they need to be warned. I appreciate your willingness to assist me, but I can't let you risk your safety for me and I honestly don't know how to begin without..." She trailed off, looking unsure.

"Without what, Veil?" he prompted.

"My necklace. My...wings," she replied, knowing that to Pete that must sound insane. To any human, it would sound utterly ridiculous. Before he could respond to this information, she continued, "I need my wings to help me to get home and possibly help me communicate with those I had to leave behind. Please, I know this sounds crazy to you—why wouldn't it? But please try to understand."

She looked at him with pleading eyes, silently begging him to absorb the information she had given him, but confusion and doubt were beginning to cloud his features.

"I am trying hard to understand, but you have to know that this does sound a little...unbelievable. I mean, you only just got here. We've only just met and now you need to leave?" His voice held an edge of suspicion.

"My family is in trouble, please don't ask me why. I can't fully explain, I just know."

Pete leaned back in his chair again, folding his arms across his chest. He looked vulnerable, yet angry and guarded at the same time. His eyes were staring just past her, his sight fixed on something beyond the door and into his living room. She moved her head slightly to try to catch his gaze but with no success. He released one of his arms from his chest and his hand reached up to scratch the stubble on his face and then rub his eyes, tired and frustrated. Blowing a long steadying breath he began again, remaining in his self-protecting position.

"I just don't understand what the big rush is? I mean, how much trouble could have occurred with you gone for, what? Three days? Can't you possibly just stay a little longer and then we'll get you back?" Pete's manner remained stern, but Veil noticed his eyes were growing desperate.

She sat back and adopted the same pose, running her fingers through her purple hair, which she had observed that morning was beginning to look pale and felt thinner.

"I have already told you I can not fully explain and to be honest it would not serve me any better in telling you, because you wouldn't believe me. It would only convince you that I don't need help and that I am crazy." She paused and looked up for his reaction, which so far remained neutral and unconvinced. She pressed on.

"I know I haven't been here long and things between you and I have, well, developed rather…rapidly?" This made her smile but when she looked up, it was not being returned. "Anyway, I can not impart any more details than I already have without endangering you, or terrifying you. Please try and understand. I have let my family down more times than I would care to remember. This is my chance not to. Please, Pete. I have to try."

He still sat, arms crossed over his chest and his expression guarded, only now he was clenching and unclenching his jaw—Veil could see the muscles working on either side of his face. His eyes looked up into hers and what she saw truly surprised her. There was disbelief, yes, but something else that could have been bordering on condemnatory. He quickly stood and walked over to the worktop where his kettle and teapot stood, his back to her as he rested his hands atop the small station, his head bent in contemplation. Veil could only watch as he stayed this way for a few moments, presumably to calm himself down or gather his thoughts. She could only hope that he would understand, although if their roles were reversed, she was not entirely convinced that she would be able to do the same. When he finally turned around, he took another long, drawn-out breath and steadied himself against the worktop, facing her. She looked at his tanned hands resting against the white marble and thought what a perfect contrast his fingers made, gripping the light surface.

"Look, Veil," Pete began, "I'm trying hard to respect that there are obviously aspects of your life that you can not share with me. But I would appreciate a little more information—a little more honesty than I am being given right now. This seems so outlandish and to be frank quite vague, so please do not judge me for running shorter on patience as you become less willing to share your story with me." He hung his head and lifted his hands in defeat before continuing.

"Veil, we've known each other just a matter of days and more than once you have come to my rescue, saved me in one way or another. But even without the dramatic circumstances in which we first met, I feel a very fierce and profound connection with you. And last night was…so…life altering that now I don't know if I can live without you. I don't want to live without you."

He lifted his head to look at her, hoping that what he had just revealed would compel her in some way to want to stay, that she would know he was being sincere and he prayed with everything he was and everything that he believed in that she would feel the same, but when she looked up at him, he saw that her eyes were empty; he had lost her, and she had made the decision to go anyway. She was going to leave him. Just as quickly as she had appeared and saved his life, she was going to leave again and destroy it. He waited for a response; when none was forthcoming he spoke again.

"Say something, Veil." When she still didn't speak, he asked again. "Say something please? Why do you have nothing to say?"

Veil remained with her gaze fixed on him, tears filling her eyes as she tried desperately not to let them fall. She couldn't explain. There was no possible way of offering any more information without Pete thinking she was crazy. His stare had grown hard and tired. Veil spoke quietly, but with conviction.

"I don't want to leave you either, Pete, and trust me, there is a connection here. Between you and me; a very deep and real connection. Please believe me when I tell you that it is unbreakable. Whether I am here with you or somewhere else, it's always been there and will remain that way." She knew this was the truth—their connection had been born before Pete was; it was a spiritual and soul-linking thread that was invincible. Though she knew her chances of convincing Pete that this was the undeniable truth were challenging at best, she prayed with every feather on her wings that deep down, his heart would believe her.

As she silently watched him, she tried to gauge his reaction, read his emotions, which was harder to do without her wings. However, Pete wore his heart on his sleeve and hiding his emotions was never an easy task. She could see it, feel it coming off him in waves; frustration, disbelief and distrust.

"How can you possibly know that? Veil?! We've known each other a matter of days! Yes, we obviously have something real and hopefully strong, but unbreakable? Without you here, if we're apart I don't see how that's possible. Our relationship would grow and become stronger if you were here, and we could explore it, deepen our apparent bond before we deem it invincible. But in order to do that you need to be with me, simple as that." His voice had grown hard and Veil desperately wanted to grin at his attempt to hold authority. If only he knew what was happening, the war that was being waged.

Pete was angry, trying so desperately to maintain some sort of control over a situation that was slipping from his grasp with every vague and indefinite answer that passed Veil's lips. He felt powerless and weak—wasn't a man supposed to help and protect the woman he loved?

"Veil, I would love nothing more than to allow my heart to be open to the mystery of what you are telling me. I wish I could believe that if you go home and I remain here you will return to me after helping your family, and that things would be the same when you're back with me…"

"I'm not sure I could come back, Pete." Veil interrupted him. "Once I am home, I'm not sure if I can ever come back." A tear fell but she wiped it away quickly with the palm of her hand.

"WHAT?" he shouted in response, his voice dripping with disbelief. "Then how did you get here?"

"By accident. I'm not supposed to be here."

"You're not supposed to be here?" he repeated it as a question to her. "Then why are you here, Veil? How did you get here? Why…why are you here?!" He slammed his hand down on the work surface and took a step towards the table where she still sat.

Veil didn't know how to answer his question without angering him further by leaving him in the dark on the details. Telling him the truth of why she was there would make this whole conversation even more unbelievable, but she couldn't lie to him. Deciding to go with the truth, although only what she thought she needed to divulge, she spoke very quietly.

"You needed me."

With that, she gently pushed herself from the table, her chair making a soft squeak against the floor as she moved to the window with her back to Pete. He watched as she retreated, stunned by what she had just said. How does someone respond to a revelation like that? He sat down, quietly waiting for further explanation from the ever more mysterious woman.

Veil stood, looking out of Pete's window into the street below. It looked just as it had in her dream. A typical Seattle autumn scene, the sun shining brightly, yet cool and crisp, with beautiful orange and brown leaves piled up on the pavements. It was a busy street, and Veil concentrated her attention on a small group of children in jackets and hats, diving into a large pile of crunchy fallen leaves on the ground, kicking them high into the air so that it looked as if it were raining leaves all around them. They giggled and shouted with pleasure and enjoyment while their mothers watched on from a nearby bus stop. Veil inhaled deeply and closed her eyes, longing for home, missing her family and the kind faces of Shye, Dusk and Kin.

"So," Pete spoke from his seat at the table, "this is on me? It's my fault that you're here?"

Veil didn't reply, instead turning her head slightly in his direction to indicate she had heard and acknowledged what he had said. She didn't want him to feel guilty; there was no fault or blame here, but she could not get the words past her lips. She once again turned her face towards the window and closed her eyes, allowing the warm sun to be absorbed by her eyelids, hoping for a quiet moment to gather her thoughts.

"It's my fault that you're here," Pete continued. "Is that what you're saying?" His tone had become accusing and suspicious. She had expected that, and waited for more, still with eyes closed, trying to remain in the moment, allowing the sun to warm her face through the glass.

"So I was in trouble and you came to rescue me? Is that what happened, Veil? What are you? Some sort of guardian angel?"

Veil internally winced at the anger in his voice. All these questions she could not answer. Keeping her eyes closed, her brows drawn in determination, she decided she would tell him what she needed to, answer his questions and then leave. She did not have time for this delay. However, when she opened her eyes again, ready to turn around, she noticed something, up far in the distance, in the perfectly clear blue sky. She could see hope in the sky, a perfect reassurance that everything was going to be OK. As relief flooded through her, she smiled fully and allowed a tear of happiness to slide down her cheek and drop from her chin. For in the blue sky in front of her, she saw a perfect, bright star and she knew what this meant. A star being born during the hours of the day meant that everything was fine, everyone must be happy. If she still had her wings, she would have felt them flutter with happiness.

Slowly she turned to Pete with a full smile on her face, keeping back the tears as she whispered.

"It's all right. Everything is going to be all right now. I can stay."

Chapter Seventeen

Shye and Dusk practically ran through Aureia heading for the healer's hut to see Kin and share their news. When they reached their destination, they were both so happy and relieved to see Kin sat up in bed, no longer displaying bruises, and nor did he bear the face of a man in pain. He still appeared tired, with black rings around his brown eyes, his mousy hair tousled, but he smiled as soon as he saw them enter the hut, hand in hand. Lorelei had her back to them as they entered; she was holding a large book and reading from it, her lips mouthing the words as she read. The small wrinkles that were these days visible around her eyes and lips had done nothing to diminish her beauty, and her blue eyes were still radiant and full of wisdom. She turned and smiled at them, her long unruly curly hair pulled up behind her; she looked like a school teacher glad to see her favourite students.

"Shye, Dusk, what are you two doing here? Everyone else is asleep."

They looked at each other and then back to their friends, both wearing large silly grins. Dusk nodded her head in the direction of Kin and giggled, indicating that Shye be the one to tell them the news. Shye nodded and stepped forward.

"We have come to seek out Lorelei's blessing to perform a very important task for us," he said mysteriously.

Lorelei closed her book and put it down behind her, but kept her eyes on Shye, cautiously stepping towards him.

"And that would be?" she enquired, though from their facial expressions she speculated it may be a task she would be more than happy to perform. Shye and Dusk glanced at one another again and then at Kin who was leaning forward, waiting with baited breath for the news to be delivered. Shye looked back to Lorelei and grabbed Dusk's hand tightly.

"We need a joining ceremony, right now," he said, a huge smile appearing on his face.

Lorelei looked from Shye to Dusk, feeling the happiness flowing from them; it was contagious and hit her like a wave, causing her to smile fully and laugh with joy, her eyes filling with tears of happiness. She clapped her hands together and then gathered them both in a giant hug, the many bangles on her wrists jangling together with her movements. She stepped back from them and wiped her tears; she could see how happy they were. Shye chuckled.

"So, you won't mind performing the ceremony then, Lorelei?"

"Have you both thoroughly considered the possible consequences of this decision? If either or you should perish whilst wearing the other's wings the other will perish also?"

Shye took a deep breath and nodded. "I have, though I endeavour not to allow that to happen," he said with conviction. Dusk nodded, indicating that she too had considered it but agreed with Shye's thinking. She wouldn't let anything happen to him or herself.

They had not yet heard from Kin, and they turned to face him. His expression was guarded and looked hurt, like he was trying to stop tears falling. Relinquishing his hold on Dusk's hand, Shye moved closer to the cot. Kin tilted his head in question, then immediately looked down to his hands resting on the thick grey blanket, his fingers fidgeting nervously. Clearing his throat before he spoke, Kin began to talk in a quiet and timid voice: "Shye, I thought you weren't gonna do this? It was too dangerous."

Shye took a long steadying breath and in an uncharacteristic display of affection he sat on the cot next to Kin, stilling his fidgeting hands with one of his larger ones. He held on, forcing Kin to look at him. When he finally looked up, there was defeat in his eyes.

"What's wrong, friend?" Shye questioned quietly.

"It's just…if anything were to happen to either of you, I'd probably be able to struggle through that. But now, if something happens to one of you I lose you both. And that is something I would never be able to cope with, I'd be alone. I guess…" He shook his head. "I'm just being selfish."

Shye squeezed Kin's hands harder and looked up to where Lorelei and Dusk stood. Dusk felt fresh tears prickling, for Kin was speaking her own fears. Lorelei was looking on, her experienced eyes full of understanding. Shye examined her for a few moments longer, hoping she would provide an answer, but she did not. She only offered a sweet smile and a gentle nod of her head. Shye looked back to his friend and spoke again with a quiet certainty.

"Kin, you are my dearest friend and you mean the world to both Dusk and me. If anything were to happen to either or both of us, I think you would cope because you are much stronger than you believe."

Kin snorted at what he saw as an attempt to make him feel better. Shye continued.

"No, really. Sol told me that you are destined for greatness and that you are an invaluable element of Aureia and its survival—whether Dusk and I are here or not is irrelevant. You will be great anyway."

Kin's eyebrows had raised and disappeared behind his hair in disbelief. Shye nodded, slowly and a smile appeared on his face.

"However, when you achieve these extraordinary feats, Dusk and I will be here to witness them, because I will not allow anything to happen to either of us."

Kin stared in wonder at Shye. With everything that was occurring in Aureia and on Earth how could he possibly know that? He needed more reassurance.

"Can you promise me, Shye?" he asked, his expression begging for comfort, for his faith to be restored. Shye studied him for what seemed a long time, the certainty he felt before slowly vanishing. He looked to Dusk for reassurance, and saw the same question in her eyes: could he promise that nothing would happen to them? He looked down and took a thoughtful breath to prepare himself and nodded assuredly. He met their gaze once more.

"Yes," he said. "Yes, I promise."

Kin and Dusk both released a sigh of relief and smiled, full beaming toothy smiles. Shye turned his attention back to Kin and returned the smile before taking on a far more serious expression.

"Kin: we not only came here to tell you of our plans, but to also ask you, well…you're our oldest and dearest friend and we wanted Lorelei to perform the ceremony, but we also wanted you to be our witness."

If it were possible, Kin's smile got even bigger. He leapt forward from his sitting position and engulfed Shye in a huge hug, squeezing him tightly. His eyes closed during the embrace and a single tear rolled down his cheek. Lorelei wrapped her arm around Dusk and squeezed affectionately as they watched the scene before them. Kin quickly wiped the lone tear away and released Shye, then sat back to look into his face; a happy grin mirrored by his two friends. Kin nodded slowly.

"Of course I'll be your witness. I'm honoured you would ask me."

"Who else would we ask?" Dusk said. She leaned into Lorelei's embrace and rested her head upon her shoulder, feeling at peace and content for the first time, knowing the other half of her soul was coming home and also that he was as elated as she was at the sudden turn of the events. She did still wonder what drastic event it was that changed his mind, but pushed the worry deep in the back of her mind, willing for just one moment of perfect happiness with Shye.

Lorelei released her and stepped into the middle of the thin scented cloud floating from the candles and filling the small hut. It smelled of cherries and menthol, and inhaling it gave a delightful tingle to the lungs, instantly settling any pain.

"When would you like this blessing to take place?" she asked them both.

Shye looked at Dusk and remembered his dream. He was not going to make her wait any longer. He would not run or hide anymore.

"Right now," he said.

Lorelei looked a little shocked, but could tell from Shye's presence that there was no alternative; it was now or never. Quickly running through in her mind the list of things she needed in order to perform the ceremony, she gave a quick nod of her head.

"OK then. Dusk, you go get ready, and Shye, you help me with your friend here." She looked to Kin sitting up excitedly in the bed. "Then we will perform your joining ceremony."

Dusk grinned and gave Shye an excited wave as she left the hut, a happy skip in her step. Shye watched her all the way, his heart feeling as though it might burst from his chest just from knowing that upon her return they would be joined, forever. Lorelei lightly tapped him on the arm to draw his attention. He turned back to her smile, affectionate and nurturing.

"Come on, Mr. Shye," she said. "Let's get your friend here out of his bed and looking a bit more decent so he can be your witness."

Shye nodded and soon enough Kin was standing. Lorelei smoothed a warm cloth over his face and arms, leaving the scent of jasmine on his skin, and although Kin must still be experiencing some pain, Shye observed that he seemed far less weary, his eyes no longer exhibiting the dark rings that they had previously. Kin's strength was returning and Shye was pleased; hopefully he could prepare himself for any trouble in the future.

Soon Kin was looking and smelling a lot better, and Shye took steps to leave the hut, but a hand grabbed his arm and stopped him, turning him around pulling his hair out from its tie. He looked at Lorelei in bewilderment as she pulled out a comb and pushed it through his chestnut locks, making them shine and wave. She picked up an aqua coloured bottle and poured a few drops from it into her hands, then rubbed them together, the jingle jangle of her bracelets filling Shye's ears as she rubbed her palms over his face and neck. He sniffed at the oil Lorelei was rubbing into him; it smelled of the ocean, with a sweet tanginess to it, and he smiled, deciding that he liked this new scent. Lorelei finished rubbing in the oil and disappeared inside a small closet space behind her cot, from where she pulled out a robe, very much in the same style as the ones they already wore, but this one was a deep orange with flecks of browns and gold.

"This is for you, Shye. I made it for you, for today," she stated as she handed it to him. Shye looked at her with questions in his eyes.

"Sol came to me years ago and told me to make this for you," she continued, "because one day you would need it. I spent months making it and even longer making Dusk hers." She smiled and Shye returned it, relieved to know that Dusk was receiving the same special treatment.

A short while later found Shye, Kin and Lorelei standing next to the Window, awaiting the arrival of Dusk. Shye looked elegantly handsome and had a glow around him as he stood with Kin to his right, both with their hands in front of them, beaming smiles upon their faces. Shye was adorned in his new robes, his wing pendant at his chest, polished and shining beautifully in the light, his glossy hair framing his face and lightly touching his shoulders. Lorelei stood before them; she had pinned up her hair, displaying her long and elegant neck that sparkled with the many small glistening diamonds encircling it and falling into the hollow of her throat. Her bright blue eyes twinkled with happiness and expectation as they faced the direction from which Dusk would emerge. They kept their gaze on that area and watched; with each second that passed, Shye became more nervous; his feet began shuffling and his hands had a slight tremble. Lorelei's hand covered his own in a bid to calm him, but she kept her gaze forward, a knowing grin on her face.

Then at last there she was. Dusk walked towards them, slowly and softly. When Shye caught the first glimpse of her he had to remind himself to resume breathing, for she was undoubtedly the most beautiful creature in the universe. She strolled towards the small group, her long blonde hair flowing behind her, swaying with her hips as she moved. She was wearing a robe similar to Shye's, although this one was paler, with hints of silver and grey, and hung low around her chest, where her pendant glistened as the rays hit it. She was smiling the most beautiful full smile, unshed tears of happiness in her eyes—eyes gazing only at Shye as she moved closer. Kin and Lorelei exchanged a smile and observed their friends with joy. As Dusk reached them, Shye brushed away an errant tear that had run down his cheek, then clasped both of Dusk's hands in his own, drawing strength from her. His trembling immediately ceased.

Lorelei looked at the couple and smiled, confident that they were doing the right thing, for she could see it in their eyes; they belonged together. In all of her time in Aureia, she had only witnessed such a connection with one other couple and although they did not have their happy ending, she felt certain that Shye and Dusk would. A joining ceremony in Aureia was always a small affair and exceptionally rare, yet one of the most powerful events that could take place, which was why she felt so humbled to have been asked to be a part of it, and as she glanced at Kin grinning from ear to ear, she knew he was feeling the same way. With satisfaction and joy filling her, Lorelei took a deep breath and began to speak.

"What a fantastic occasion and what a truly incredible couple. Shye and Dusk: you are two of the bravest, kindest, most honest and extraordinary Guardians I have ever had the privilege of knowing and watching grow here in Aureia." She looked over them both; they each glanced back at her and grinned.

"We all know that falling in love is often not an easy task. There are obstacles, challenges and unfortunately others will try to drive you apart. But you must remain strong together, prepared for anything that you may face, with your hands linked and hearts beating as one."

Shye and Dusk both gave a slight nod at this and smiled in agreement, each sharing determination to follow through on that statement.

"It is a ritual in Aureia, when you join with another that you exchange wings—the symbols that hang above your heart, and it is a demonstration of your commitment and a reminder that you are carrying a piece of that other person with you, forever. This exchange also means that if either of you should fall in battle, on Earth or anywhere else, with or without the other, they too will fall and both shall perish. Do you both understand the weight of this responsibility and accept it?"

Shye nodded. "I do."

Dusk also nodded and gripped Shye's hands tighter before she echoed his response. Lorelei smiled and continued.

"Now, if you would both remove your wings?"

Both Shye and Dusk reached behind their necks and unclasped their pendants, each feeling the unnatural lightness around their chests.

"Dusk, would you please place your wings around Shye's neck and make your vow."

Dusk nodded, took a small step closer to Shye and stood on her tiptoes so she could reach around his neck. Her hands caught in his hair and he smiled and moved it aside for her. She securely clasped the ends of the chain behind his neck, gently running her fingers across his jaw as she withdrew. Shye shivered at her touch. Dusk's wings were far less heavy than his own—more delicate yet with an underlying strength. Dusk looked into his eyes as she began to speak.

"Shye, you are the bravest, sweetest, proudest and most stubborn Guardian I have ever met. We have known each other a long time and for every second of that time I have been yours. I don't know why you came to me tonight and brought us here, but whatever the reason I am eternally grateful. I promise to be with you forever and I will always be a friend to you, love you and protect you with my heart, my wings and my life, for the rest of our time together. Whether that is decades or moments or somewhere in between, they will all be special because they will be with you. I would love nothing more than to live my life falling asleep in your arms every night and waking up in them every morning."

Dusk finished her vow. She had spoken confidently and with conviction throughout, and Shye stared back at her in wonderment, amazed at the words that had fallen from her lips. He felt very humbled; that someone he found to be so incredible would have those thoughts about him. He opened his mouth to speak, but nothing came out. Dusk was looking at him with a twinkle in her eye, knowing she had flustered him and caught him off guard. Lorelei watched with some amusement; Shye the great warrior, was tongue-tied.

"Shye?" she grinned, her voice full of mirth. "Would you now place your wings around Dusk's neck and speak your vow?"

Shye looked at her and then back to the woman standing in front of him. He gave a slight nod and stepped forward. As he moved, Dusk reached up and swept up her long hair, exposing a long elegant neck and expanse of flawless creamy skin. Shye swallowed as he caught the scent that was all Dusk, the sweet smell of honey and fresh air, and though he was a great warrior and defender, skilful with a sword and an expert in combat, his hands shook, his large fingers struggling with the delicate clasp as he tried to secure it around Dusk's neck. He held his breath until he eventually fastened the ends together, then stepped back, expelling the air he had been holding. Dusk was smiling at him with nothing but love shining in her eyes; he hoped he was mirroring it as he spoke.

"Dusk, I was worried I would not be able to find the words to tell you how I feel and promise you the things people do when making their vow. But I suspect you, like others before us, have just spoken the truth, so I'll try that. When I am not with you, I only feel like half of a person, like my heart isn't beating all of its beats and I want to feel every heartbeat with you." Shye paused and took a breath, uncertain that what he wanted to say was coming out right, but then he felt Dusk squeeze both his hands and he continued.

"All I have ever wanted is to have you by my side. I want to be your friend, companion and more than anything I want to protect you. I would never let anything happen to you because my world, my whole existence would mean nothing if you were missing from it. You are an excellent Guardian, you're amazingly kind, funny and the way you talk of your love for me is quite often, overwhelming...and every breath I have is yours now forever because every day you rob me of it. I look forward to every day, forever."

Shye finished with a soft smile, but Dusk was grinning ear to ear with tears of joy running down her cheeks. Lorelei was also smiling and had unshed happy tears in her eyes. She cleared her throat ready to formalise their exchange of vows.

"The Guardians before me have exchanged wings and spoken their vows to one another, with Kindred, a fellow Guardian, as their witness. Kindred, do you acknowledge that Shye and Dusk have exchanged vows and wings here today?"

"I do," he responded with a big smile.

Lorelei nodded in acceptance of his statement.

"By making this vow to one another, you have linked your hearts, souls and wings. You will now grow together, adding more light and warmth into your lives. You will now grow together and into one another. Therefore, in the realm of Aureia and being surrounded by the spirit of Sol, I declare that Shye and Dusk are now joined. May it be forever so." Lorelei finished with an almost cheeky grin. Shye stared at her expectantly and she indicated to Dusk with a nod of her head. Shye was still wondering what was to happen next and looked at her in confusion. Lorelei sighed in exasperation and looked to Dusk for help, even though she was trying hard to refrain from giggling. Eventually Dusk took the initiative, knowing as she did that Shye was clueless when it came to much of what was involved in love or displays of affection. She gently grabbed both sides of his face and brought his lips down to her own before he could ponder or protest. His eyes immediately widened, but then closed as he fell into the kiss. Dusk dropped her hands from his face and placed them around his back in order to bring their bodies closer. Shye did the same and soon there wasn't an inch between them as they shared a gentle yet powerful kiss. As they stood connected, a white glow began to surround them, growing brighter and brighter until they were no longer visible.

The light became so intense and bright that Aureia was filled with its warmth, as it touched every inch of the ground, filtering into the small windows and inside the huts, where Guardians awoke from their slumber as they were drawn to its source. Slowly, more and more Guardians gathered around the light, allowing the glorious heat to bathe their faces, all of them now wearing the same beaming smile as they realised where the light and warmth was emanating from. As Shye and Dusk slowly pulled apart, the glow around them dimmed and as it dissipated they saw the entire population of Aureia gathered around their ceremony. They looked around at all of the familiar and happy faces and smiled at them in return. Suddenly someone clapped their hands together and Shye and Dusk spun around to find that it was Kin who had begun clapping. Now everyone else followed suit—all of Aureia was clapping and cheering in celebration for Shye and Dusk. They looked back at Lorelei in amazement. She too was clapping. She placed two fingers in her mouth and whistled loudly.

Amidst the applause, Shye and Dusk gazed upon each other, moving forward until their foreheads rested against one another. Shye closed his eyes, basking in the sensation of Dusk being so close.

"We did it," he whispered.

Dusk giggled and replied, "Finally!"

Chapter Eighteen

Veil had been stood watching Pete, seeing only hurt and confusion in his face. Now she turned her attention back to outside of his window, smiling as she looked up into the clear crisp blue of the sky. She didn't know if anyone else could see it, but she knew exactly what she was looking at. It had no place in that sky but there it was, with the perfect blue as a backdrop: a star. Or rather it looked like a star, but Veil knew that she was looking at a joining ceremony. When two Guardians are joined they create radiant glow around them so bright that they almost disappear as it swallows them, as if their happiness is visible on the outside as they make their vow to one another. But more than this, Veil knew, deep down in her heart that she was looking at her friends.

Shye and Dusk had finally been joined. She didn't fully understand how she knew—she could just feel them, as if she were there with them. The tears that left her eyes were of happiness, sheer joy that her friends had exchanged their wings. She also knew that she was not dreaming, for this was not like the other nightmares she had suffered during her time on Earth with Pete. The bad dreams had seemed like warnings or threats, whereas what she was witnessing now was a great moment and one she felt confident would not have taken place in Aureia if it were in any immediate danger. She knew that Shye would not join with Dusk if they were under any degree of threat, because his main focus would have been protecting Aureia and those within it. It was this that had allowed Veil to determine that her family and her home weren't in any danger—they couldn't be or she would not be witnessing the miracle in front of her in the sky. She heard Pete clear his throat and tilted her head over her shoulder to indicate she was listening to him.

"You can stay?" he asked doubtfully, although she could hear the note of hope in his question.

She turned from the window and looked at him, smiling and wiping her tears from her face and nodded. When she looked back through the window the small star had disappeared but she still felt the same happiness that she had when she first saw it.

"Yes, Pete, everything is going to be OK. I can stay here with you. I want to stay here with you." She took a few steps towards him.

"What's changed, Veil? In a matter of seconds?" He moved forward to meet her in the middle of the room.

They were just a few feet apart now, each looking at the other with questions in their eyes. Veil slowly reached out and took Pete's hands in her own, her thumbs gently stroking the skin. Pete looked down at their hands, daring to hope that this turn of events was genuine. He felt that connection again, the bond between them growing stronger and the incredible tingle shooting up his arms as a result of Veil's fingers against his skin. He kept his gaze down and whispered.

"How do you know everything will be OK, Veil?"

Veil could feel Pete's hands shaking within her own, and thought carefully about how to answer. It was both important and very challenging to answer his questions without divulging too much, without frightening him and yet satisfy his curiosity. She felt elated that Aureia was safe; her dream must have been nothing more than her own mind scaring her for being away from Aureia. She ducked her head in order to regain eye contact with Pete before she spoke. His deep brown eyes were filled with doubt but also a sparkle of hope that this was real. Veil took a steadying breath.

"Because I believe it will be," she answered with conviction.

Pete frowned heavily in confusion and he continued looking at her, hoping that she would elaborate.

"Pete, there are things in this world that are hard to explain, sometimes impossible to explain and sometimes I wish that this was not so, but I see no other option if I am to keep you safe and sane. I am asking you to trust me. Please believe that I don't wish to be anywhere else but by your side." She gazed into his eyes, hoping he would find the truth of her words laid bare.

Nodding slightly, Pete dropped his hands from Veil's and placed them around her waist, pulling her in for a fierce hug. Veil felt the love she had for him fill her entire body as she breathed him in and held him close, feeling his slightly scratchy face against her own and hearing him breathing in her scent. She could not hide anymore; would not hide anymore. He deserved more than that after what she had put him through. Turning her head, she brushed his ear with her lips.

"I love you," she whispered.

Pete looked up and smiled the biggest smile she had ever seen from him.

"I love you too, Veil," he whispered back.

Slowly they moved towards each other, eyes closed as they shared a gentle, exploring kiss and clung to one another. When they broke apart, Veil all of a sudden felt bashful with Pete's eyes upon her. He was like an excited young boy, bursting with giddiness.

"We need to celebrate!" he exclaimed.

Veil giggled and looked at him questioningly.

"I'm taking you out tonight and we are going have a great time," he said. "However, I think we need to get you some new clothes. I think you look great in mine but you need something more...girly?"

Veil just shrugged. She liked wearing Pete's clothes because they smelled like him; talcum powder and aftershave. But she also liked the idea of wearing something Pete found her more attractive in. She nodded and smiled.

"Ok then," he began. "Why don't you use the bathroom and get cleaned up, then I'll take you shopping in town?"

Again Veil nodded and walked past him, stopping to give him a peck on the cheek before heading for the bathroom. Once there and with her clothes removed, she took the opportunity to examine herself in the small mirror. She reached up and gently swept her hair away from her back so she could look upon her wings. She had to crane her neck uncomfortably to see, and panicked briefly when she saw nothing but an expanse of smooth skin, but then she saw that at the base of her back were a few remaining feathers, no more than twelve or so and the tips of them were faded, as if they were slowly disappearing from her and yet her skin felt as if it were absorbing every last one. She smiled, feeling settled and content at the thought of spending the day with Pete, and every day after, for this was what she had always wanted. She brushed her teeth, ran a comb through her hair and did a small skip on her way out of the bathroom.

She returned to the living room and found Pete sat on the edge of his sofa, his arms folded, looking comfortable and relaxed. A ray of sunlight was highlighting his eyes, his expression of open adoration as he looked at her and held out his hand for her to take. They walked down his hallway and he opened the front door.

"Are you ready?" he asked.

Veil took a deep breath, nodded and squeezed his hand, knowing as they left his apartment that this was going to be her first day as a woman in love with no fears, doubts or obligations to anything or anyone else and she was going to revel in every second of it.

Chapter Nineteen

All of the Guardians were gathered; in small and large groups rejoicing at the event of the couple's joining. Shye and Dusk stood with Kin, some patting him on the back while others expressed their congratulations to the happy couple. They smiled and laughed along with their friends and throughout the conversations and wishes of happiness they remained close together and their fingers stayed linked. Lorelei was alone in the crowd, watching from a distance, enjoying the peace for a little while, for she could feel in her heart that it would not last long; she shared a special gift with a few others that gave them a partial link to events yet to pass, although on days like this it was more like a curse. She closed her eyes, silently wishing that they could all have a little longer before their happiness was to be disturbed. As she opened her eyes again, she saw a flash of dark purple in front of her and that tremble of impending doom landed in the pit of her stomach before she heard the clapping.

Everyone turned at the sound of the slow, unenthusiastic applause to see Veil making her way through the crowd. Her wings had lost a lot of feathers, and appeared weak and lifeless; her purple eyes were now black with no pupil and no glint of life in them; her hair hung thin and greasy around her face. She ceased her clapping and tilted her head to the side, grinning viciously.

"Well, well, well," she addressed Shye. "If I'd have known I'd have brought a gift."

She advanced on them and Shye stepped in front of Dusk and Kin to protect them. He no longer knew Veil, even though she was his friend—a friend who had invaded his dreams, threatening Dusk's life in exchange for information that he didn't have. But as he looked at her now, he didn't see Veil standing before him; he saw an imitation of her. Taking a few small steps forward, he examined her more closely, her skin was pale and cracked around her lips and eyes, her finger nails were too long and sharply pointed, her bare feet appeared dirty and her whole being seemed unstable and forced somehow. They stood a few feet from one another.

"Who are you?" Shye asked.

There were gasps from the crowd around them. Dusk and Kin took a step forward; they too now looked at Veil with questions in their eyes.

"Finally begun to connect the dots, have we, kids?" Veil asked.

"I asked you a question," Shye said firmly.

"That you did, boy. And believe me, you don't want an answer."

Shye took another step closer.

"Believe me, whoever you are, I will have answers and I don't care what has to be done or how long it takes to get them." He took a deep breath and felt that the person in front of him already knew what he was going to ask. "Where is Veil?"

The groups of Guardians around him were utterly bewildered and their whispers of confusion rose up as Shye and the girl stared at one another. She smiled and began to slowly circle around him, then closed her eyes and took a long deep breath before returning his gaze.

144

"She is safe and far from here."

"How is it that you have her wings? Why is her pendant around your neck?" Shye tracked her movements around him.

The girl reached up and sneered as she touched the wings on her chest. She hated them. They felt like a weight dragging her down.

"Because I took them from her," she replied staring deep into his eyes. It was inevitable—that he would hate her once he found out, that he would just wish for the real Veil to be returned—yet somehow she felt unprepared and saddened by it, though would never let it show on her face. She kept her cold façade and continued.

"During the hours of night and under a cover of rain I took her wings and stole her identity in order to infiltrate Aureia and gain the information I was sent for." She stopped pacing and turned her face away to avoid his glare.

"What information was that? How to control the Knights?"

"Yes."

Shye stepped back and pushed a hand through his hair. "Assuming you had gained this information, what use could this possibly have for you?"

"The information was not for me, but for my master."

She looked up, knowing this was the moment that it would all change. It was the beginning of the end and she realised deep down that she was standing on the wrong end of this interrogation. She wanted to be next to Shye, not questioned by him. But still she remained passive and braced herself for the arrest and onslaught that was to befall her.

Shye was standing close now, breathing heavily, rage burning his eyes. He towered over her and she looked to her feet. She could feel his breath, feel him trembling as he tightened his hands into fists. Leaning in a little he asked her quietly, "Who is your master?" He shut his eyes awaiting the answer, but he knew it without her needing to say it. She had also closed her eyes and now she stepped back from him. She reached up to the heavy pendant around her neck and removed it, lifting it over her head. At the last touch of metal against her skin, a cloud of black mist surrounded her. Shye backed off and stood to shield Dusk from whatever was about to happen. The mist began to move over the form of the standing girl, becoming thicker and thicker, swirling from her head to feet. It smelled of smoke after a fire and gave off coldness. It lasted only a few moments yet it seemed to take forever to disperse and once it had there, stood before them, was a different girl. Surprised cries and gasps erupted throughout the crowd and some were screaming. Shye looked on in disbelief and felt Dusk's hand take his own. Kin took his place beside Shye, his face fixed in an expression of shock.

This new girl had black hair with red tips and roots, her eyes were hard, shiny black with a hint of red. Her features were harsher than Veil's and she was shorter and stronger in appearance. She wore all black, but her clothes were ripped in places and she had several piercings in her ears and one in her nose. She looked back up at Shye with hollow eyes, her dark pointed teeth on display. She held her arm out straight with Veil's wings dangling from her fingers and continued to look at him as she spoke in a more shaky tone now.

"My master's name," she dropped the wings to the floor, "is Vulgaar."

As the last word escaped her mouth, Shye ran at her in a rampage, yelling in fury and knocking her to the ground. The breath left her lungs and she yelped at the impact of her back hitting the floor. Before she had even a moment to think about what was happening, Shye turned her onto her stomach and lifted her hair from her neck. He saw it and quickly scrambled from her, his eyes wide in disbelief. The other Guardians crowded around and looked down on the girl who remained in the position for them all to see the evidence of who she was. Everyone was shocked and some close to tears, for underneath her hair and central on the back of neck was a dark V shaped tattoo, the letter swirled with intricate dots lining one side. It was the mark of Vulgaar—proof of what she was.

"You're a Draxyl," Shye stated, his voice husky with bewilderment and a little wonder at the discovery. How could he have not known? This girl didn't impersonate Veil well at all. That bewilderment quickly turned to anger with her and with himself. He grabbed her by her arm and forced her to stand up. When she did, she saw the eyes of every Guardian on her, hurt, shocked and disapproving. She tried to remain defiant, but failed when she saw Shye bend down and retrieve the wings pendant that she had dropped moments before, his eyes filled with sadness and worry.

"What did you do?" he asked quietly. Dusk watched on silently, though she could feel Shye's anger from where she stood. The girl did not answer.

"WHAT DID YOU DO?!" Shye shouted so loudly that even the girl in front of him was startled. He was in her personal space, his face inches from hers, and she was reminded, momentarily, of Vulgaar. Shye's presence so close was just as intimidating and he towered over her.

"What's your name?" he asked her in a cold voice, lacking any emotion now.

"Lash," she answered, keeping her face turned to the ground. "My name is Lash."

Shye nodded at this information, taking a little step back but still remaining close to her. "Now, Lash, what did you do to Veil?"

Everyone waited in silence. Lash glanced around the crowd at all of the eyes, watching her expectantly, and returned her gaze to Shye, finding nothing but cold indifference. When she spoke again she could hear regret and shame in her own voice.

"During the fire at the hospital. Vulgaar saw the love that Veil had for Dr. Pete Standon when she saved him from the building. So, that night, he ordered three Draxyls to attack him, knowing that Veil would break all and any barriers in order to save him, including flying down alone in the dark. I have to admit I was very impressed, she is a good fighter."

Lash paused and lowered her eyes from Shye. "She was completely unaware of my presence and I hit her from behind. She went down and my friends and I continued to beat to kick her." She dared to look up for a brief moment and although Shye's face was unmoving, his eyes now held a terrifying rage. She could feel it coming from him, aimed at her.

"Go on," he demanded.

"The element we had not imagined is that Pete Standon would be brave enough to try and save her, for that is what he did. He couldn't move so he threw his drink can at us. It cracked and the fluid went into my comrades' eyes. They stumbled and we ceased our blows. Vulgaar then made it rain. He made it rain so hard that we became invisible to Pete and everyone else. I took Veil's wings from around her neck while she was unconscious."

Lash scanned the crowd again and noticed the disgust on everyone's faces, Shye's was still angry yet neutral. Behind him Dusk seemed to be waiting patiently for the rest of the story, while next to her Kin looked petrified. Shye crossed his arms over his chest, perhaps to restrain himself from attacking the girl in front of him.

"How is it that you look like Veil?"

Lash held her hands out, palms up in a gesture like surrender. She shook her head slightly from side to side.

"I'm not sure. I am the only Draxyl to have these...gifts? I can change form. I'm very strong and I can hear things that are very far away. Vulgaar has told me that he has never known a Draxyl to have such abilities." Her voice sounded smaller as she mentioned Vulgaar.

Shye nodded but kept his arms folded across his chest. He cleared his throat. "And how did you get here?"

Lash bit her lip nervously as she considered this question. Eventually she shrugged. "I think Veil's wings guided me here. My plan was once the wings had emerged from my back that I was going to start flying in hopes of finding Aureia, but I didn't really have control over where they took me. I was just kind of drawn here."

Again Shye nodded and turned to some of the Guardians around him, seeing that they shared his feeling of anger for this woman. They were all looking to him for answers, for guidance, as if he were the only one able to make this better. The weight of the responsibility hit him hard and forced him to avoid their gaze, He pinched the bridge of his nose between his fingers, considering his next move. Just a short while ago he was as happy as anyone could be and now he felt as if the fate of Aureia was resting on his shoulders— perhaps on the next few words that would leave his mouth. He dropped his hand from his face and looked up, hoping that Sol would say something to him, but he heard nothing; just the hammering of his own heart. He felt Dusk's fingers curl around his own, and when he looked at her he saw understanding. She smiled softly at him.

"Whatever you want to do next, I'm with you. No matter what."

"Me too." Kin stepped out from behind Dusk.

Shye nodded, in that moment feeling eternally grateful to have Dusk, and such a wonderful friend in Kin also. He turned back to Lash, who appeared defiant and angry, yet Shye detected remorse and regret also. Behind her the Guardians stood strong and fast, looking to him for an order. He took a deep breath and returned his gaze to Lash, staring her straight in the eye.

"Restrain the girl," he commanded, noting the shock register in her eyes as the two Guardians grabbed her from behind and kept her still. She fought and growled at them, displaying her sharp teeth, gnashing and biting at them.

"Take her to Unenda and bind her there."

As the Guardians nodded and dragged her away, Lash looked back over her shoulder, her black eyes boring into Shye and causing a terrifying chill to run up his spine. He took a deep steadying breath, then turned to Dusk and the remaining Guardians so they could all see his face as he addressed them.

"Do not approach the Draxyl! She is to remain bound and ignored until I return. Do you all understand?"

They all nodded to signal their agreement, except Dusk.

"Where are you going?" she asked.

"To find Veil," Shye said, taking her hands and smiling to reassure her. "To find Veil and bring her home."

Chapter Twenty

It was a beautiful afternoon; the sun was shining and the sky was clear. Shye had returned to the small space of the city in which Veil had been tricked and attacked. He wore blue jeans and a black t-shirt, his long hair tied back, a few strands falling over his face. He surveyed the area in front of him; there was a small shop with a bell that jingled when the door opened. Shye closed his eyes and tuned in to the sound of that bell, focusing on the image that formed in his mind, of Pete leaving the store with a heavy, tired footfall, into the dark and almost deserted street. When he opened his eyes again, he saw bright sunlight against the windows of the shop and a smiling clerk behind the counter. He crossed the street and looked at the pavement, immediately noticing the stains of a liquid having been spilt. Again he closed his eyes and saw the beer cans hitting the ground, spraying out in all directions.

Back in the sunshine, squinting against the sun, he thought back over the last few hours—his terrible nightmare, exchanging wings with Dusk and telling her how he felt, but damn, how good that had felt. He reached up and smiled as he traced the new wings hanging above his heart, more delicate than his own, yet as he touched them he felt the connection with Dusk and it gave him further strength and encouragement.

As he walked away from the shop and the fluid on the floor, he felt a pull in the other direction, almost as if an invisible force had given his hand a little tug. He turned to follow with eyes closed and saw Pete, soaked to the skin, lifting Veil's broken, beaten body, and in that moment Shye could feel Pete's protectiveness of her, and he could smell lavender, the smell of Veil. It made Shye a little happier to know that she was with someone who was willing to protect her at any cost; it was a rare thing, especially amongst the people on Earth; but Pete Standon was different.

Following the route that the unseen power was taking him, the scent of Veil became stronger, and Shye was almost running to keep up with the tug on his hand. He passed multiple doorways and trees and plenty of people that he almost knocked over in his efforts to get to wherever it was he was going, round corner after corner until suddenly he found himself on a very busy high street, filled with hundreds of people all in as much of a rush as he was, overwhelmed by the murmurs of all the voices being carried and the closeness of bodies as they scurried past. He was trying hard to avoid stepping on anyone's feet, becoming increasingly impatient and frustrated by those who simply stopped in front of him to answer their mobile phone or check on a tourist map that they were in the right place. Someone bumped right into him, making him stumble and he had to quickly shift his weight to avoid a fall. He looked back over his shoulder. A man in a dark coat turned his head and Shye was startled by what he saw. The man's eyes were black and his smile was cruel, and though he also looked a little sunburnt, it was clear to Shye that he was looking into the face of a Draxyl. Now he remembered what Lash had disclosed—that Draxyls did not like the sunlight but could tolerate it.

As Shye tried to continue onward, it became a frequent episode; more and more people were colliding with him, each of them bearing the same dark eyes and menacing smiles. He felt a sinking feeling in the pit of his stomach and decided to cross the street to try and escape the people mass, but as he took a step from the pavement a black van screeched to a halt in front of him, the large side door already open and hands reaching from it, They grabbed him by the arms and shoulders, dragging him into the van and then took off at high speed, tyres smoking and screeching.

Without even so much as a moment to process what was happening, fists and feet rained down on Shye's body. He grunted and groaned as each blow hit him, trying to keep his wits about him. There was enough light in the van for him to see that there were at least six Draxyls attacking him, all of them big and incredibly strong. He could see their eyes, their teeth and the tattoos on the back of their necks as they swung their whole body into each strike. He could also smell smoke on their dark clothes, like they had been on fire and instantly extinguished. Even though the space was small, Shye did his best to gain leverage on his attackers and even managed to strike back against them, punching two of them in the ribs and face, sending them flying backwards, winded and holding their torsos in pain. The others were becoming tired, the unsteady movements and swerving of the van proving too difficult for them to hit accurately. Shye stayed still for a moment, letting them believe he had been beaten. The largest of the Draxyls was bald, with tattoos on his face and neck. He leaned towards Shye, panting in his face with breath that smelled of burning metal. He ran a finger across the wings that hung from Shye's neck.

"When your girl comes down here looking for you," he sneered, his voice thick and full of hatred, "she will get far worse than this."

The other Draxyls laughed, like hyenas cackling along with a pack leader. Shye's eyes became hard as stone and he focused them on the big bald one speaking to him, watching him laugh, feeling a deep rage welling within him, giving him power. They continued to laugh as the biggest one continued.

"I have a message from Vulgaar for you, cloud rider."

Shye turned his face upward, letting him know he was listening, but remained calm, giving the slightest nod of his head. The Draxyl wiped the sweat from his top lip with his sleeve and spat on the floor. He knelt down to maintain eye contact and then said in a harsh whisper, "You're never leaving this van." He burst into laughter again, his comrades joining in and doubling over, slapping their knees and each others' backs.

Shye reached up and touched Dusk's wings around his neck, closing his eyes and breathing deeply. This wrath he felt building in him was terrifying, but fuelling his desire to survive and protect her. As they continued laughing he slowly got to his knees, acting as if he were in pain, then, before any of them saw him move, he pinned the Draxyl that spoke to him against the side of the van, the swerving was making it difficult to hold him steady but he did and he got nose to nose with him.

"I have a message for Vulgaar," he hissed.

He grabbed his attacker by the scruff and threw him from one side of the van to the other. The other Draxyls were stumbling and falling over as Shye continued to thrust him from side to side. It was taking every ounce of strength he had inside him; in his hands, arms, and in his heart and soul. The driver of the van shouted a warning behind him, the wheels of each side lifting from the ground as they careered along the street at speed. The Draxyl had lost consciousness, but Shye didn't care. He kept on going and with one last yell and push, the van rolled causing everyone to tumble onto the side that was now sliding along the ground, the metal screeching and screaming as it scraped against the road.

The Draxyls were all unconscious, but Shye was not, and as he looked up he saw they were heading at speed towards the back of a truck and other vehicles in a line of traffic. He reached up to his wings of Dusk's pendant and held onto them until the last moment before impact, hitting them against his chest and causing them to emit a bright light that filled the back of the van and shattered the windscreen. A second later, the black van made contact with truck, both exploding instantaneously.

Shye was not inside.

Chapter Twenty-One

Veil had never been so happy, never felt so light-hearted as she did walking along the high street holding hands with Pete and looking for clothes in store windows. She had already purchased a short but elegant dress in the most wondrous dark purple fabric that shimmered in the light. What she liked most about the dress was the way Pete's face lit up as she stepped out of the changing room, like a little boy on his birthday. As she tried on the abundance of outfits and surveyed herself in the full length mirrors, twirling to see her back, she noticed that more feathers had disintegrated from the tattoo, now only a few remaining at the bottom of the right wing and they too were fading fast. She was scared yet also elated by the sight, for it signified the disappearing link between herself and Aureia, each lost feather another step closer to her new life beginning on Earth, with Pete.

After the purchase of that first dress, Pete informed her that it simply was not enough; she would need shoes and jewellery and eventually everyday wear. So they continued to stroll through many streets, peering inside every shop and stopping off for coffee and a snack. As they walked, holding hands, Veil broached the subject of money.

"Once I have figured out what I am going to do here I promise to repay you."

Pete smiled at her and shook his head.

"That's not an issue, Veil, but what do you think you may want to do? What did you do before?"

Veil thought for a moment.

"I protected people, helped them out of difficult or dangerous situations."

Pete nodded, having become accustomed to Veil's cryptic way of speaking about her past. He gave her hand a squeeze and smiled.

"Kind of like police or paramedics?" he asked.

"Exactly like that!" Veil said, nodding enthusiastically. She grabbed Pete's arm and leaned her head on his shoulder, relieved that he understood without having to explain anymore. He thought a little longer and then grinned at her.

"Well, we could enrol you in an academy to retrain if you need to?"

Veil smiled. How considerate Pete was to want to help her choose a career. She stood on her tiptoes and gave him a peck on the cheek. It would be nice to do the jobs she had done before on a permanent basis; she loved to help people. She let the thoughts fill her mind as they continued their walk, but as they turned a corner they were confronted with the sight of a massive traffic accident and an array of blue flashing lights. Pete quickened his pace, now close enough to make out the remains of a black van underneath a truck and several more cars crumpled against each other. Pete went straight to a paramedic.

"I'm a doctor. Is there anything I can do?"

The paramedic shook his head and reassured Pete it was all under control. The van was found without anyone in it and the truck driver had abandoned the vehicle when he saw the van heading for him. Veil took the scene in with horror and a sense of utter helplessness, an unsettling familiarity falling over her like a dark blanket. Feeling as though she were being watched, she looked up quickly and saw paramedics, police and fire crew looking right at her. They had all ceased what they were doing, dropped their instruments and stared at her in wonder.

Veil recognised them immediately. They were Guardians and they were seeing her for who she really was. She ran towards them, to reassure them, to tell them she was all right and everything was going to be OK. A group of people crossed her path making her stop in her tracks. She tried to peer over their heads to maintain visual contact with them but once the crowd had passed the emergency crew that had been watching her had disappeared. The few that remained paid no attention to her; they were humans getting on with their job, and the Guardians had vanished before she could speak to them.

Pete returned to her side and wrapped his arm around her shoulders.

"You OK?" he asked.

"Yes..." She shook off the feeling and smiled reassuringly. "Yes I'm fine."

Pete wasn't convinced. Veil seemed really shaken up from viewing the accident.

"You sure?"

Veil nodded again and grabbed his hand that was hanging over her shoulder.

"Yes, I just...I thought I saw someone I knew."

***

Shye lay on a cot in Lorelei's hut, inhaling her enchanted candles. They were rapidly healing the pain in his face and sides where he had been punched and kicked. Dusk was at his side, holding his hand, as he retold the story of the Draxyls in the van. He noticed that of all who

159

listened to his tale Lorelei was the most shaken by it. She seemed deeply traumatised and Shye could see she was trying to distract herself by tending to him. The candles she had lit were good for healing bruises and swelling; they smelled of apples and cinnamon, giving Shye great comfort.

Suddenly a small group of Guardians appeared at Lorelei's doorway, out of breath and panicked. Shye sat up.

"What's wrong?" he asked. "What is it?"

Dusk turned to look at them; Lorelei too was waiting anxiously.

One of them—a young man with black hair and piercing blue eyes—stepped into the hut, nervously looking from Lorelei to Dusk before settling his gaze on Shye. He cleared his throat and was still a little out of breath.

"It's Veil," he said. "We found Veil."

Chapter Twenty-Two

Shye, Dusk and Kin now stood at Unenda with a few others. Shye stood at the front, his arms folded across his chest, his face sporting only a few bruises now from his attack in the van. He was glaring at Lash. She was tied up and pinned to the bricks of the never-ending tower. Her head was bowed and her eyes were closed. Everyone had assumed she was sleeping, but Shye knew; she was praying. She was praying for Vulgaar to rescue her. He could see her lips moving as she begged silently for him to save her and Shye could sense the waves of heart-shattering disappointment emanating from her because he hadn't. It was a foreign concept to Shye but feeling Lash's pain gave him some comfort. He cleared his throat to try and get her attention but still she did not move. Instead he spoke in a loud and clear voice so he knew she could hear him.

"Vulgaar is not coming for you. He is ignoring you."

That got her attention. Lash's head jerked up whipping her red hair away from her face. She narrowed her eyes and stared back at Shye. He looked smug, even though he had taken a good beating.

"You try to find the girl?" she asked, cocking her head to the side as she took in Shye's injuries.

Shye nodded and took a step closer.

"But your friends found me first."

Lash gave a little chuckle; how foolish they all were. She let her head fall forward again. She was losing energy fast. Shye clapped his hands in front of her face to wake her up again.

"Do you know why Vulgaar wants to control the Knights?"

Lash felt herself slipping away, as though she were disappearing. Everything became fuzzy and she tried to scream, shout, to tell them that she was leaving her body. Her eyes closed and her body trembled once more, then her head fell forward. She was motionless.

Shye stepped closer, searching for a sign that she was alive. She was still breathing—long, drawn-out breaths—but was otherwise limp and lifeless. He looked back to Dusk, his arms falling to his sides, defeated. She was still watching Lash, a worried expression on her face. She nodded at Shye to prompt him to act. He turned his attention once more on Lash and began reaching a hand out towards her head. All of a sudden she looked up, tilting her head from side to side, peering curiously at him; as if she had never seen him before.

"Lash?"

She shook her head, no.

Shye stepped back, observing this new turn of events. Lash's face, features and body were still here, but her spirit was not. The presence dwelling within her now was powerful, dangerous and looked predatory. Shye swallowed hard and examined her more carefully. The eyes, although still black, had aged by centuries and he sensed they held many secrets to the universe within them. He felt the same power in this being that he felt when Sol spoke to him, only this power was dark and malevolent with nothing good in it.

"Vulgaar?"

162

This time the girl nodded and smiled at him. Even the smile was different now, it was a bigger, fuller smile and the most disturbing he had ever encountered. The person in front of him spoke.

"Who's a clever boy then? No wonder you're Sol's pet."

The voice was not Lash's. It was a deep, raspy, masculine voice but with Lash's underneath it, like she was an echo of what Vulgaar was saying. Vulgaar chuckled with his teeth exposed and it sent chills through Shye and he guessed through everyone behind him, for they had all taken several paces back from the being tied in front of them.

Shye took stock of the situation; if Vulgaar could escape and hurt them he probably would have by now. Maybe because he was using Lash's body as a vessel he was no stronger than she was. Shye decided to try and gain some information.

"What do you want?" he asked.

Lash's eyes glanced up to where the top of the tower would be if it were visible, and the body took a big dramatic sigh. The black eyes refocused on Shye.

"I want control of the Knights of the Sun." The voice was still deep and intimidating but now held an air of co-operation.

"Why?"

The face looked incredulous. It snorted as if it would be obvious.

"Because they are the strongest and most powerful warriors to have ever existed. They would be a tremendous asset to any cause or army."

"But you know they only answer to the requests of Sol. They are fiercely loyal to her. So what good would it do you?"

"How do you know they are loyal to Sol?"

Shye thought for a moment. How did he know? He'd never seen them—only heard Sol speak of them. As he continued to think of an answer the being in front of him began to chuckle once again.

"You see, boy, they are only serving her because they have never been offered an alternative."

Shye looked at him in disbelief. "Nothing is ever that simple."

The face looked at him inquisitively and shrugged. "Everyone has the capability to choose sides; to change paths…for the right price."

Shye didn't want to believe that. The other Guardians were looking just as horrified by this mad man's twisted logic. The Knights of the Sun were as old as the Sun itself and had been loyal to Sol since their creation. Shye stood his ground. He stepped forward with purpose and kept eye contact with Vulgaar.

"Not everyone."

"Oh yes, boy. Everyone and anyone would choose a darker path that led to life and victory if the alternative led to death and failure. Even you."

Shye's eyes flared with anger and he moved so he stood directly in front of Vulgaar.

"Never," he said with a conviction deep within him.

He looked back to Dusk to see her watching him with eyes full of pride. He smiled at her, then turned back to the figure tied before him.

"My patience is wearing thin," he said.

The figure no longer appeared indifferent or co-operative, just bored and restless.

"Forget about the girl left on Earth. Worry not about the Knights. Once I have what I want, you can all choose the side you want to fight on. Though I promise you, if you stay here it won't end well for you."

Shye stood over him, looking down into his eyes, trying to appear authoritative, though actually fearing the presence below him. The face sneered hatefully.

"Stay out of this, boy. We've already won this fight."

"You've never seen us in a fight!" Shye countered.

The face looked taken aback for a moment, then began laughing, the voices of Vulgaar and Lash overlapping in a disturbing cackle.

Shye moved away from the horrible noise and returned to Dusk's side, seeking her hand in comfort. The ground started to tremble under their feet, and the bricks of Unenda began to rattle and move. Everyone stepped back as the tower very slowly inched its way closer to the ground.

The body tied to it began to struggle violently and look to the Guardians for help, but they all just watched on motionless, too scared to move. Suddenly a scream erupted from its mouth, a blood curdling scream that carried throughout Aureia as the being disappeared in a cloud of black smoke. Lash's body was gone.

The ground began to shudder more violently and the tower continued to lower into the ground. Clouds of dust were rising from the rapid shaking movement and the Guardians all ran away from it. Once they were at a safe distance, they stopped and observed what was happening. For what seemed an eternity the tower shrank down through the ground and the heat of the implosion reached them, flowing around them and through them. Shye thought if it were this warm and they were this far away, close up it must be too hot to stand.

Suddenly the shaking stopped and the clouds of dust settled, revealing an open doorway in the tower. A burning bright light emerged from it and the Guardians all hid their eyes. Shye used his hand as a shield and squinted at the doorway, seeing the silhouette of four enormous figures coming towards them on equally enormous horses and armed with weapons and shields. They continued to move towards the Guardians, who watched on in awe and made utterances of wonder as the figures slowly became clear.

They rode in a straight line, the first on the left was riding a brown horse with white markings on its legs. He was a striking man with long flowing blonde waves of hair and orange eyes, a very square jaw line and a serious expression of determination. He carried a shield that depicted a fire being extinguished by rain and an axe was attached to his hip. The second man was much stockier with shorter red hair and a long beard. Again his eyes were orange, though not as startling as the first man's, and he didn't look serious. If anything, he appeared rather joyful and fully proud to be up on his light red-tan horse. His shield displayed a younger man with similar features holding a spear and smiling. Third in was a dark looking man with tanned skin and eyes more golden than orange. His hair was thick and black, falling to just below his ears, his chin dark with stubble. On his back was a powerful bow and arrows. His shield bore the mark of the sun and the stars in one sky, and his expression was one of intrigue. He continued to look from side to side, watching for any presence or danger, and the dark brown horse he was riding appeared to be doing the same. The final man of the four, riding on the right, was the biggest of them all and the most striking. He appeared older, with grey hair and stubble on his face and neck, but he also seemed the strongest. He looked truly commanding and heroic, with an impressive sword at his side, though his shield was bare.

As the four riders grew closer to the Guardians their size became more apparent. They were now a few feet away from the crowd, and their horses stood taller than even Shye. The man on the right ushered his beautiful white horse to take a few steps closer and he addressed them all, but kept his gaze on Shye.

"I am Morningtide," he told them in a voice full of authority and experience. "The man next to me is Justice."

The dark man with the arrows nodded to the group.

"Next to him is Ignatius."

The red-headed man with the beard nodded and gave them a warm smile.

"And finally, Antemeridian."

The man with long blonde hair looked upon them but gave no other acknowledgement.

Shye stared up in wonder. These four warriors were an incredible sight to behold. They exuded confidence, power and valour. He returned his gaze to Morningtide expectantly. Morningtide nodded.

"We are the Knights of the Sun."

There were gasps around the gathering of Guardians, but Shye waited for the next statement, the one he had predicted would fill him with dread. Morningtide looked to him and then the rest of them before speaking again.

"We have been summoned by Sol to prepare for battle tonight."

The crowd erupted with cries and shrieks of fear and disbelief, murmuring of impossibility and being outnumbered. Even Dusk and Kin looked doubtful.

The Knights observed, unsurprised though disappointed by this reaction. Shye stepped away from the crowd and shouted, "HEY!"

Everyone, including the Knights, paid him their fullest attention.

"Vulgaar and the Draxyls plan on stealing our days, our very sunlight! The essence of who we are and what we defend is under threat, right now. The Knights are here to help us and if we fight with everything we have, we can win this! We can take our sunlight back! We can scare them away and make sure they NEVER return. We have to take the fight to them, we have to get Veil back and we will not surrender into the darkness or let them hide under a cover of rain. But the five of us cannot do it alone."

Shye glanced at Morningtide, who gave him a nod of respect. He looked once more to the crowd. Dusk take a step forward and smiled at him. Kin followed, then a few more, and a few more, until every Guardian had formed a line of soldiers willing to fight alongside him. Feeling pride swell within him, Shye turned back to the Knights.

"We'd better be ready. It's getting dark."

Chapter Twenty-Three

Veil gripped Pete's hand tighter as he led her into the club full of dancing bodies. She was wearing her new dress, a little make-up and had freshly washed and blow-dried hair. Pete had surprised her with a necklace he purchased while she was finishing eating her lunch. It was a silver wing on a very long chain and looked nothing like her own but still brought her some comfort as it hung near her tummy and tapped against her as she moved. She was so nervous walking into this place, never having been near anywhere remotely like this before but still excited to be here with Pete as her guide. He was wearing a dark blue shirt and smart black trousers. He had dabbed expensive cologne on his neck and Veil thought he was looking and smelling very sexy.

Pete pulled her towards the bar to order a drink. While Pete spoke to the barman, Veil allowed herself to fully view her surroundings. The club was dark with only a few coloured lights dotted around and a small number of tables and chairs, but the dance space was the biggest aspect and it was filled with people moving excitedly in time with the music; everyone was up and dancing.

"Here you go," Pete said, handing her the drink. Veil took a small sip. The drink was orange and fruity with a very potent kick to it and she liked it very much. As she continued to sip, she felt Pete settle in beside her, bottle of beer in hand, and allowed the steady beat of the music to take her over.

The band on the small stage were young men, the bass was low and deep, the rhythm coursing through her body and causing her to tap her foot in time with it. The lead singer had a clean, sexy voice and sang about angels emerging from the clouds and into the sunlight, but it didn't sound divine. To Veil's ears it sounded seductive. She grabbed Pete's hand and they moved to the dance floor, immediately putting their arms around one another to bring them closer. They were surrounded by sweaty, gyrating bodies, moving along to the addictive beat. Veil found her hips swaying with Pete's, her nails digging into his shoulders, his lips press against her neck…

***

Shye stood with Dusk at the Window. They were now in their armour—Shye in dark gold and Dusk in silver. An army of Guardians were aligned and ready for the battle, some were fearless; others were shaking or laughing nervously. The Knights were speaking with Sol alone and far away from Shye's ears. He wasn't thrilled about it. He'd hoped that Sol would seek him out to give him hope before the battle, although he felt better for having Dusk at his side. They both looked down on Veil, in the club, dancing with Pete. They had spent so long trying to locate her, but Morningtide had a stronger link with everything and everyone on Earth and had found her immediately.

"I think we're ready," Shye said.

"Me too," Dusk agreed.

They briefly held hands and then turned to command the force behind them. Shye took a deep breath and spoke loud enough for all to hear.

"It is dark down there—something we are unfamiliar with. But we are stronger, we are faster and we are going to win!"

A cheer erupted and the Guardians held up their hands and weapons in agreement.

"Keep your wits about you, stay fast and come home safe."

He turned back to the Window.

"NOW!"

***

Veil could feel the little alcohol she had consumed trickling through her veins. The beat of the music was in time with her heart and she and Pete were as close together as it was possible to be. The bodies around them were doing the same, feeling the music and feeling alive.

***

The Guardians flew down in a gliding, exquisite line towards Earth. Their wings were all extended as they soared with purpose, into the night to save Veil.

***

Veil and Pete moved as one on the dance floor. She felt tingling all over her body where Pete touched her, completely enthralled by the music and his presence so close to her. The song changed pace, now faster and heavier, making them move faster without realising. Then, just as it was about to end, the front door of the club burst open and there stood a police officer flanked by others. Everyone in the club scattered as the team of police strode into the club.

171

"This is a raid! Everybody out!" the frontmost officer shouted and everyone ran out of the doors.

Everyone, that is, except for Veil—and Pete, who wouldn't leave without her. Veil stood still in shock, for she immediately recognised the police officer shouting for everyone to leave. It was Shye. He slowly moved towards her and smiled. She ran to him, leaping into his arms and he wrapped them around her, squeezing so tightly, inhaling her lavender scent. He slowly released her and as her feet touched the ground she turned to see Pete looking confused.

"Pete, this is my...brother, Shye. Shye, this is Pete."

Pete extended his hand, but Shye shook Veil's arm to get her attention.

"We've no time for introductions, Veil. You have to come with me. Now."

He started to pull her outside, where it had started raining. Pete trailed after them.

"Veil who is this man? Please tell me what's going on?"

Veil was still being pulled along and trying to resist.

"Shye, stop! I'm staying here with Pete! Stop it! I'm staying."

Shye continued striding forward, a firm grip on Veil's arm. A little further away from the club, they turned into an alley, and Veil saw that all the Guardians were assembled, stood lining the alley, rain dripping from their faces and fear in their eyes, along with strength, prepared for whatever was about to happen. As Shye turned to explain to her, he was distracted by a noise from above him. He looked up and sighed resignedly.

"It's too late. They're here."

Chapter Twenty-Four

Vulgaar stood at his ledge with an army of thousands of Draxyls behind him and Lash at his side. They wore no armour, carried no weapons and had no fear on their faces. Thunder clapped above their heads in the skies of Stormcry. Vulgaar smiled as he watched the scene below—Shye trying to save Veil and the doctor. He concentrated on them and made it rain harder, made the thunder so loud they could feel it.

How sure he was that he was going to win this fight. He could feel his own power, his hate for those below him thrumming through his veins. This battle seemed tedious—only a handful of cloud riders against his vast army. He felt her presence by his side: his most gifted creation; the one able to change form and manipulate anyone near her.

Lash observed the scene with dread. Although she had deceived the Guardians, she wanted nothing more now than to help them. Shye had shown her a warmth and goodness that she feared she would now never know. She did not desire victory or power. All she wanted was a friend. But she was chained to Vulgaar and until she could find a way to become unchained, she had no choice but to do his bidding.

"What are you going to do?" she asked without looking at him.

Vulgaar turned to her and grinned, then looked down again.

"Really make it rain."

Chapter Twenty-Five

"It's too late. They're here," Shye said, looking up in panic. Veil and Pete looked up too, as did every Guardian. Through the rain they could see Draxyls teeming through the formidable clouds above. Hundreds of thousands of bodies were falling from the sky and attaching themselves to the surrounding buildings. Through the stinging rain they could be seen crawling down buildings like spiders and they were moving so rapidly. Soon they had almost covered the expanse of the buildings, so many dark shadowy figures scaling down every side and corner of the apartment buildings then leaping down into the alley below.

Shye put his arm across Veil and Pete and pushed them against the wall, slamming their backs to the wet bricks. Pete looked up in horror and though he couldn't identify the beings crawling towards them he immediately feared them, yet felt protected by the army of police surrounding them in the alleyway.

"GET READY!" Shye shouted over the loud, torrential rain and the thunder clapping over head. He turned to Veil and Pete, then reached up and hit his wings to his chest. In a blindingly bright flash of light he was in his gold armour, a red handled gold sword hanging from his hip. Pete's eyes widened in amazement, not just at the sudden transformation from an ordinary police uniform into full body armour. What really made him gasp were the wings that had expanded behind Shye. They were huge and magnificent. Pete watched in astonishment as the girl next to him did the same, the blast of bright light revealing a female warrior in silver armour, her wings slightly smaller but no less amazing. It went on, down the line on their side of the alley and opposite them, small blasts of light as one by one each Guardian hit their wings to their chests and then stood proud and strong, with fluttering wings and armoured for a war. They were now an army of Angels.

Shye looked at Veil and then back to the creatures coming for them. He gave her the slightest smile, understanding her plight a little better after his dream involving Dusk.

"Join us or get to safety with Pete." As he said it he opened her hand and placed her wings in her palm. As soon as the metal touched her skin she felt complete, the connection between herself and Aureia and between herself and her brothers and sisters standing in the alley returning immediately. They had risked everything to come here and save her. She looked to Pete who was staring at her in confusion, and yet she sensed he understood.

"I have to go," she told him.

He nodded, his blue shirt soaked through, the rain dripping from his eyelashes and lips.

"I know," he said.

Veil put her wings around her neck and closed her eyes, gasping as the incredible warm and familiar sensation swept through her. Looking into Pete's eyes, she reached up and pushed her wings against her heart. He watched, astounded, as Veil emerged from the light and her wings opened up, extending to their full size. She took a deep, satisfied breath in and opened her eyes, meeting Pete's gaze again. She was no longer the Veil who had been shopping with him, or dancing in his arms. She was where she was supposed to be; she was home.

"Get to safety," she told him. Pete nodded and ran away from the alley.

Veil stood next to Shye and leaned around him to see Dusk, staring up at the sky, fear in her eyes. The Draxyls were getting close. Veil had no armour, but Shye reached for her hand and put a sword in it. She continued to watch above her, the Draxyls now jumping from roof to roof and making their way down to the ground. Shye stayed very still, taking deep breaths and preparing to give the order. He wanted them in the centre of the space so the Guardians could attack from both sides. A few Draxyls dwindled down, then a few more and soon there were a hundred menacing creatures staring at the Guardians with hate and rage in their eyes. They carried knives, rocks and broken glass. The rain was pouring down on them, but they seemed to love it, as if Vulgaar were rewarding them for fighting in his name. They licked their lips and fidgeted restlessly, waiting for the first move.

Shye watched them and slowly raised his sword over his head.

"ATTACK!"

The Guardians swarmed in from each side, wielding their swords and screaming battle cries. The Draxyls swung their weapons, scratched and clawed, gnawed and bit at their enemies. More and more Draxyls were joining in the fight, jumping from the buildings they were climbing, leaping from rooftops and landing right in the middle of the action. Shye was swinging his sword and moving too quickly for any Draxyl to gain an advantage; he swung and ducked between any blows and weapons. He had slain at least forty yet the battle was becoming more and more of a struggle. He quickly glanced to Dusk to see she was doing just as well, impressively missing strikes and delivering quick blows. But they were now outnumbered by fifty or more to one.

Veil was fighting with everything she had. She thrust her sword, using its handle to knock enemies away from her and jumping high in the air to strike them from above, but she found herself drowning in the sheer number of them. There were ten of them all coming at her with rocks and glass, kicking and punching her and she was knocked to the floor. As she lay there, looking up through the rain at the Draxyl now advancing on her, she recognised that it was Lash standing over her, the one who had stolen her identity, staring down at her, the expression on her face completely unreadable. All of a sudden Lash was also knocked to the floor and she lay there motionless. Veil looked up to see Pete standing there, holding a small shield. Veil got to her feet.

"Thank you," she said. "Now get to safety and stay there, I'll be back. I promise."

Pete nodded and squeezed her hand before running away for a second time. Veil looked back to the battle and saw only dark figures in the rain, struggling to see any Guardians now. They were losing and she could feel her world ending. But then she spotted a light in the distance, a bright, orange glow, moving slowly at first, then faster, getting closer and closer to the scene of the battle. Soon it was above their heads and within it she saw four men on horseback wielding their weapons.

Everyone stopped their fighting to look up at the riders; the Draxyls looked petrified and the Guardians looked relieved. Antemeridian lifted his axe high above his head and shouted to the battle below.

"TO THE SKIES!"

The four riders turned and started to ride their horses upwards into the clouds. The Guardians all simultaneously bent their knees and took off after the Knights, soaring with their wings. The Draxyls growled in rage and jumped back onto their buildings, quickly crawling up them to catch up with the Guardians, then floating away from the structures, towards the scene where the Guardians and Knights hovered, waiting.

The Guardians were now on one side of the sky and the Draxyls the other. The Knights of the Sun were behind the Guardians, their horses pounding their powerful hooves against the clouds. The Draxyls stood in their thousands with only a few hundred Guardians opposing them. The Draxyls snarled and started running at their enemy. The Knights waited for the Guardians to run first and then broke into a gallop, their weapons swinging in front of them. There was a clash of swords against rocks and spears, Draxyls and Guardians both screaming with fear and determination. The battle raged on, but with the Knights fighting alongside them, the Guardians now had the advantage. They wiped out twenty Draxyls with one swipe of their weapons and their horses chased them away by the hundreds. Shye began to believe that they could win, that they were going to win the battle of the sky. He looked to see Dusk looking right back at him, she smiled and held up her sword to him. But then Shye saw her expression change; panic filled her eyes and she started flying towards him very fast, knocking him down and confusing him. He heard her cry out in pain, quickly turned her over and saw it: an arrow had hit her chest. He looked up to see a Draxyl with a bow drawn, for a moment looking directly at him, before it turned and fled. Shye turned back to Dusk; she was bleeding and fading fast. He shook his head in horror at the realisation.

"What did you do?" he cried.

"I couldn't let it happen to you, I just couldn't. I'm so sorry." She wept in his arms. Shye's tears began rolling down his cheeks. "Shye, I'm scared."

Shye was scared too. He let out a small cry and brought their foreheads together as he looked into her eyes and tried his best to reassure her.

"It's OK," he told her. "We'll be together soon, remember? I have your wings, I'll see you soon, I promise. I'll see you soon."

Dusk looked up at him. She barely had the strength to speak, but loaded her words into an expelled breath. "You promise? Really? I'll see you soon?"

Shye nodded. He gently ran his fingertips across her face. "Really. I promise. You can go now, Dusk, it's OK. Please don't be afraid, be brave for me now. I'll be with you. You can go now."

Dusk closed her eyes, a smile on her face. Shye held her and felt her stop breathing and slip away. He held her tighter and screamed until his lungs hurt, sobbing as he rocked her back and forth in his lap, waiting to be taken as well. He buried his head in her hair and smelled…nothing. There was nothing anymore, she had gone. Gently, he placed his lips to her forehead and squeezed his eyes shut as tears spilled out.

When he finally looked up, he saw in amazement that the battle had stopped. No, not stopped. Frozen. Draxyls, Guardians, Knights—it had all frozen in time. No one was moving yet they were still in their fighting and defending stances, in mid-attack.

He was so confused and in so much pain, but then he felt the warm glow of Sol's presence surrounding him. A strikingly beautiful woman appeared before him; her eyes

180

were deep gold and her features were strong, her very long dreadlocked blonde hair swept up yet still tumbling down to her feet. She wore a yellow gown and held her hands in front of her. Shye's tears continued as she smiled down at him.

"We've lost her."

Sol nodded and took a few steps closer.

"We've lost the battle; we can't win without her. I don't care if we win without her and if I go too we'll surely lose."

"Young Shye, sometimes there is no victory in winning a battle; but victory in fighting it."

Shye nodded and looked down at Dusk. He wanted to be with her now. He cared no more for this battle or this world. He gently let go of her and she continued to float in the same place as he crossed her hands over her chest. He leaned down and kissed her cheek.

"I'll see you soon," he whispered. He knelt in front of Sol and looked into her face, awed by the beauty and power he found. "It's all right. I can go now. I'm ready." .

"Yes," she said. "Yes you are." She stepped forward and gently placed her hand on his head. She closed her eyes and there was an explosion of light so bright that it filled the entire sky.

Chapter Twenty-Six

The battle was still going on, all were becoming tired and angry. The Knights continued to fight, rescuing countless Guardians from the attacks and more and more Draxyls were falling back. Kin was fighting very bravely and with great skill, showing no fear to his enemies, yelling with each thrust of his sword to intimidate them. But someone very strong grabbed him from behind, and another emerged and took his sword. Soon there were ten or more circling him as he struggled in vain to break free. The one that had grabbed his sword came close to him and raised it above his head.

"Nighty night," he said in a cruel and quiet voice.

They all turned to the sound of a horse galloping towards them—a black stallion with gold eyes, the rider surrounded by an almost blinding glow, concealing his identity. They Draxyls raised their arms to shield their eyes from the glare and saw the swing of a sword, fleeing from Kin and the Knight that had suddenly appeared. He chased them a few paces before turning back to Kin, who was still shading his eyes from the brightness around the Knight in front of him.

"Thank you," he said to the rider.

He got no response and could only see the outline of the Knight, but then something caught his eye. The shield that the Knight was carrying looked familiar. Kin looked up and, seeing no objection from the silhouette, took a few cautious steps forward and inspected it more closely. He gasped as he realised what he was seeing on the shield. It was Dusk. His friend was engraved into the shield and she looked heartbroken. Above her face was an arrow and the word 'Forever' underneath it. Kin looked up to the Knight, seeing the tears in his eyes. Shye was riding the horse; he was a Knight of the Sun. Kin was confused by Shye's new appearance; his armour was now a brilliant, gleaming gold. His sword was also gold and not dull, and he appeared a few feet taller. His chest, arms and neck looked thicker, he no longer wore wings above his heart and his hair was down, flowing around his face. And that face looked as heartbroken as Dusk's on his shield. He offered Kin a small smile.

"She was trying to protect me," he said sadly. "That's why our shields have engravings: to tell our story."

Kin did not understand this. He felt pity for his friend not being able to join his love after she had fallen, but he couldn't say anything. Silent tears fell from his face as he continued to look up at Shye in awe of his new divine, majestic presence but also at the pain etched into his face. Shye nodded at him and cleared his throat.

"I don't understand either. I should have been with her now, but Sol made me a Knight."

Just then a scream erupted and they both looked to see Draxyls retreating from the battle as the other Knights galloped towards them, chasing them away. Shye looked back at Kin one last time and took off after his new, smaller, band of brothers. Kin could only watch him go as the Guardians began to holler and cheer at the Draxyls retreating to Stormcry. Veil came up beside him, smiling at their victory as they watched the five Knights run every Draxyl away from them.

"Who is that?" she asked.

He turned to her, with fresh tears in his eyes. Her smile immediately fell and she wrapped an arm around him as he put a hand to his eyes trying to wipe away the tears.

"Kin? What it is? What's wrong?" she asked, kissing his head and holding him close.

He turned his face away and surveyed the scene around them. A few Guardians were injured but overall they happily floated where they were, their wings keeping them in the sky. He looked at Veil again and took a deep breath.

"That was Shye. He's a Knight of the Sun. Dusk was killed in battle, trying to save him."

Veil gasped, and felt her heart break. She watched Shye in his new role, commanding and brave, she saw the pain in his eyes and Dusk's wings hanging from his sword handle. A life without Dusk for him was going to be torturous. She thought of Pete and what he had done for her tonight. She wanted to see him more than anything. She kissed Kin on the cheek.

"Everything will be all right," she said. "You have greatness inside of you. Everything is going to be all right again."

"How do you know?"

She looked into his eyes and grasped both of his shoulders.

"Because I believe it will be and belief can be a very powerful thing." She smiled and soared back to Earth as the first lights of day were breaking across the sky.

Chapter Twenty-Seven

The Guardians had returned to Aureia and the Knights with them. Shye observed them from his new perspective; he felt much stronger and faster. More than that he felt indestructible, although this new power was irreversible, and he still had questions that needed answering. He saw Morningtide outside of the celebrating group and watching reverently, so he trotted over on his horse and stopped next to him. Morningtide smiled at him; Shye noticed for the first time just how much older he looked. There was mainly grey in his hair and in his beard but also deep wrinkles around his eyes that strangely, still sparkled with youth.

"How do you feel?" he asked Shye.

"I'm not sure. I feel numb, I think." He cast a look to Dusk on his shield.

Morningtide nodded and turned his attention back to the scene of the Guardians celebrating, hugging and regaling tales from the battle. Shye cleared his throat.

"How did you feel?" he asked.

Morningtide took a deep breath and concentrated on how to answer his new brother.

"Same as you—numb, angry, hurt and confused. But eventually you start to feel again and it all helps you to become a great warrior. Being a Knight is precious and vitally important, Shye. You are to be a great asset in our forthcoming battles and struggles. We are lucky to have you on our side and this pain you are feeling will pass."

Shye nodded. Deep down he didn't want this; he was supposed to be with Dusk now. He glanced down at her on his shield and smiled, then looked to Morningtide's shield. It was duller than his own and bore no picture or symbol. As he was about to ask why, Morningtide answered him.

"I have no story to tell."

He rode away from Shye, towards the other Knights and smiled, listening to their tales of the battle they had just won. Shye was disturbed from his thoughts by the sound of his name being whispered and looked over his shoulder to see Sol standing in the distance. He rode over to her, appreciating this new sensation of invincibility and having the horse as his new companion. As he approached Sol she looked at him with a peaceful smile on her face. He slid sideways on his new saddle and jumped down from the horse, gently patting its neck as he slowly walked forward. Sol was strikingly beautiful and her calmness unnerved him. She seemed to be waiting for him to speak first.

"Did you know this would happen?" he asked.

Sol nodded.

"Why didn't you tell me?"

"Because you would never have told her how you felt about her. You would have both fought this battle without the love of the other."

"But it was a waste! You used her death to gain what you wanted from me!" he accused, the rage returning to his heart and his veins. Sol remained silent. "Would she have died anyway?"

Sol did not answer.

"Did you kill her?"

"No," she answered firmly.

"I don't want to be your Knight, Sol. Please just send me to Dusk. Please, I beg you..." Shye began to cry. Sol remained silent.

"Please, Sol, let me be with her. Please, please send me to her. I promised her I'd see her soon. She's waiting for me, please!" He was begging but still Sol's face remained neutral. "SEND ME BACK!" he shouted at her.

"I can not, Shye. This is your destiny."

Shye glared at her a moment longer, then nodded, wiping the tears from his face as he turned and walked back to his horse. As he mounted his new steed he looked down to where Sol had been standing, now just the afterglow of her presence, but he knew she could still hear him.

"I'll make my own destiny," he said to the empty space. He turned and rode away from Aureia.

Chapter Twenty-Eight

Kin stood alone at the Window, watching the sunrise light up the buildings and trees on Earth. He was thinking about how the people on Earth would wake up that morning with no idea how close they came to losing the sunshine and their freedom. He took a deep breath and thought of Dusk. He missed her so much already. As the sadness descended on him, he felt a strange warmth touch his back, roaming across his muscles and coming to a rest in the middle, above his heart. He began to turn around but was stopped by a soft yet commanding voice.

"Do not turn around, Kindred. You shall hurt your eyes."

Kin did as he was told and stayed still, knowing that it was Sol who was speaking to him.

"Kindred, you are a brave Guardian, capable of many great things. This world is better for having you in it."

He immediately shook his head, about to protest but Sol spoke again as if reading his thoughts.

"I know you doubt what I am saying, but in time you will see how powerful you are."

He lowered his head and thought of Shye and Dusk; her death made him feel empty.

"I don't feel powerful," he said in a quiet voice.

"I understand, but power can lie unknown forever without cause to bring it forth. You are courageous, strong and have a very noble heart."

Kin held his breath as the warmth at his back grew like a caress, spreading across his neck and shoulders. He had experienced this warmth before, this power. On the day the Draxyls attacked him in the street and he was rescued, he felt this heat from the inside out. It was an incredible feeling and one he hoped to become accustomed to.

"You, Kindred, are to be assigned to guard and protect someone very special and important. Are you up to this task?"

Was he? He had only just fought in his first battle and he couldn't protect himself against the Draxyls in the street that day. But his friend had sacrificed her life and been so brave. Shye was now a Knight and he wanted to believe what Sol was telling him. Could he be destined for greatness? After thinking of all these things Kin nodded.

"I am," he confirmed.

"Then look into a room in Raphael's hospital, where you will see a baby girl being born."

Kin zeroed his vision onto the building, aglow with the sun hitting the bricks. His gaze travelled along the windows and into the room where he saw a beautiful, perfect baby girl being taken from between the legs of an equally beautiful woman with rosy cheeks, beads of sweat around her brow from exertion. The mother cried with happiness and kissed her husband's hand. The husband was handsome with a chiselled face and big blue eyes. The mother had pale skin and long flowing red hair that was the colour of a sunset.

The doctor held the baby girl up and they both cried and kissed on the lips. Kin watched the baby carefully as she was wrapped up and taken to a small cot, watching all of the movement of people bustling around her. She did not cry, but gave a small contented smile as she was laid in her mother's arms. Kin watched the event take place and felt his heart swell with love and protectiveness. He felt blessed that he would be given the honour of protecting something so magical. And that is how he already thought of the baby girl: magical.

"Her name is Emily."

Kin smiled so broadly and cried so hard that he felt the muscles of his face grow sore. The warmth at his back disappeared and left him to watch this new precious bundle be placed back into the arms of her mother as her father stroked her head. Kin saw her eyes for the first time; they were a perfect clear blue and looked right at her parents with love and trust.

"Emily," Kin said. "I won't let anything happen to you."

Chapter Twenty-Nine

Veil was back in Pete's apartment, watching out of the large windows in his living room. It was still relatively early and the sun was rising across the city, an orange glow beginning to climb the walls of Pete's building. There was a woman jogging across the street, her ponytail bouncing as she went, the trees were being kissed by the early sunlight and a breeze gently moved the branches. Veil sighed contentedly; she was beginning to love this building, this street and everything else that encompassed Pete's life. She picked up a dark throw from the couch; it was itchy but warm and comforting, she covered her shoulders and arms with it and continued to gaze at the morning.

She heard his footsteps approaching the area she was standing in, the steps pausing a few feet away from her. She turned her head in his direction but didn't look at him. His footsteps continued and stopped directly behind her, his hands sliding around her waist as his arms hugged her to him, her back to his front. She felt him rest his chin on her shoulder and reached up a hand to caress his cheek, feeling him smile against her fingers. They spent a few moments just enjoying one another's presence, then Pete inhaled deeply and spoke.

"So, you were like...my guardian angel?" he asked quietly.

Veil nodded. "Though we don't really call ourselves angels. We're just known as Guardians. We are assigned to protect someone on Earth and I was your Guardian."

"I see," he replied. "That man, Shye, isn't really your brother, is he?"

Veil thought for a second before answering.

"Yes and no. Up there we are a family but he isn't a Guardian anymore. He is now a Knight of the Sun, one of Sol's chosen few. If we were going to call Sol anything, I suppose she is our mother—a goddess." She was amazed that he was taking this all so well.

"OK, so how long have you been my Guardian? Since I was born?"

"No, actually. Since you became a doctor. Sol had me watch you graduate from medical school and told me you were going to make a difference to the world. When a Guardian first sees their chosen, an overwhelming protectiveness comes over us, a newborn need to keep you all safe. But when I first saw you, I felt drawn to you. I wanted to know you and be with you and I haven't thought of anything else since.

"While I have been here with you, Pete, my wings have imprinted in my back in order to remind me of Aureia and my family there. But the more I fell for you, the more my wings faded. I have lost that part of myself because I believe I was meant to stay here with you."

"So you fell in love with me?" he asked.

Veil nodded again and brushed her fingers along his cheek.

"Does that happen a lot?"

"No. In fact it's forbidden. I shouldn't have even flown down in the dark to rescue you. It was a trap."

"Forbidden, eh?" he said with a grin and wiggled his eyebrows.

196

Veil laughed and turned to face him.

"That's all you picked up from what I said?"

"No. I'm sorry. Who set the trap? Who were you fighting with?"

There was no going back now. Pete obviously wanted to know everything and he deserved the truth.

"The trap was set by Vulgaar. He is the ruler of a land called Stormcry. We are Guardians and soldiers in the name of Sol. He has an army of thousands and they are called Draxyls. It was a few of them that attacked you to lure me down to Earth. We are forbidden to fly during hours of the night, for that is their time, but they knew I would do anything to keep you safe. After I came down to rescue you and got myself beaten to a pulp, a Draxyl named Lash took my wings and entered Aureia looking like me."

Veil felt Pete shiver. This was a lot for him to process. She waited patiently for him to speak.

"I don't ever want to think of anything bad happening to you, Veil. You mean too much to me. I promise I will do everything in my power to keep you safe. You've been protecting me for years, I think it's time I repaid the favour." Pete spoke with such conviction, it made it easy for Veil to believe she could do this; she could stay here with him.

Turning in his arms, she reached her hands up and using her fingertips she examined his face, eyes, cheeks and lips before placing her mouth against his in a sweet and promising kiss.

"Do you have any regrets?" he asked.

Veil smiled at him and kissed him again. "Not one."

He smiled fully at her and then turned towards the kitchen as she returned to watching from the window. She looked up into the sky, now perfectly calm and clear. She wondered who would be looking through the Window, and how Kin was coping with the death of Dusk. Reaching up she felt her wings around her neck. They felt different now. They lacked the power they once held. As she looked into the sunshine, her smile faded and her eyes filled with doubt. On the base of her back, one feather remained.

Chapter Thirty

Shye found himself shaking, actually shaking. He was a Knight of the Sun and yet felt a terrible fear within him, a fear almost as potent as his grief. He was in totally unfamiliar territory, a place he had sworn never to enter and now he could see why. This realm was terrifying and hideously dark. He stood out like a torch beam in a dark cave and could feel all eyes on him. It was cold here—something he was unaccustomed to—but refused to wrap his arms around himself. He was sat upon a sharp boulder in Stormcry, running his fingers over Dusk's face on his shield.

Vulgaar was standing near him, masking his smug face with sympathy as he finished listening to Shye's story. Shye dropped his shaking hands and stood, facing away from Vulgaar. He felt a cold hand touch his shoulder. When he turned, Vulgaar looked at him with a small smile and understanding in his eyes.

"Sol knew this would happen, didn't she?" Shye asked, not looking at the Stormlord. He found Vulgaar's eyes too dark and penetrating so averted his gaze when possible.

"Indeed she did, my boy. Sol is a wonderful goddess and very powerful. But she is also calculating and for many years has been known to manipulate events and time in order to obtain what she wants for her own advantage. Unfortunately in this case, you are what she wanted and, my poor boy, she has made you pay the ultimate price."

As Vulgaar finished speaking he looked to the shield that Shye carried.

"I trusted her. More than I've trusted anyone. All of this—you, Veil, Kin—was it all part of this plan? Did she know all of this would happen?"

Vulgaar nodded slowly. "Sol has the gift of vision. She can not see everything that will come to pass, but she can see the end result. If that outcome is to her advantage then she will influence certain events to make sure it will not be prevented or to ensure it will come to pass, claiming it as 'destiny'."

Shye listened and with each word spoken he became more angry. How could Sol allow this to happen? Dusk was the most wonderful, brave and caring of them all and Sol had willed her to die. He stood abruptly and almost knocked Vulgaar down in the process. His sheer size amazed the lord. Shye was now an awesomely powerful being. Vulgaar stared at him in wonder and thought of all the ways this boy was going to be of use to him. What an ally he was recruiting! Shye spun round, anger flowing from him.

"I told her! I told her I don't believe in destiny! If I hadn't let her convince me, then Dusk would still be alive. It's just so…unfair."

"Yes, boy! It is unfair. None of this is right and she will continue to manoeuvre the events of time in order to obtain who and whatever she wants. Unless we stop her."

"What do you mean?" Shye asked.

"All I want is the power that you hold, and the others like you, Shye. If I had control of the Knights, I wouldn't ask anything of you other than loyalty. I can reunite you with those lost and I would only use you if necessary. You wouldn't be banished to a tower until I called upon you. You would be free."

Shye grew quiet. It sounded so simple. So fair.

"I trusted Sol. She said we would be together forever."

"And you can be, Shye. I can make that happen for you—for both of you." As Vulgaar said this, he and Shye directed their vision to Dusk's face on the shield. She had a single tear sliding down her cheek.

"So," Shye began to ask, "you can bring her back?"

Vulgaar nodded and turned Shye, guiding him deeper into his realm.

"Yes, Shye. I can bring her back—for a price."

Chapter Thirty-One

Sol stood atop Unenda with Morningtide by her side. He held the handle of his sword with both hands and looked out over Aureia. From here, the entire realm was visible to them. It all seemed so peaceful, that stretch of time after a battle where everyone is happy to have survived to tell one another stories of their victories, no matter how small. They were both thinking of Shye: he had disappeared after speaking with Sol, concerning them both. After a long silence, Morningtide spoke.

"The boy grieves, Priestess."

Sol slightly inclined her head towards him. His eyes swept over her beautiful hair, thick with golden dreadlocks, and her long elegant neck. That warmth began to surface, that feeling of safety and love between them. She looked into his eyes, and spoke softly.

"I know. In time it will heal."

Morningtide nodded silently, maintaining the eye contact and looking over her face. He smiled and dropped his gaze, allowing her warmth and presence to wash over his soul as he waited for her to speak.

"Vulgaar will try again. He will not stop and his numbers and strength only grow," she said, her voice tinged with fear but still strong and full of conviction. "We are going to need help."

Morningtide looked up at her, questioning an surprised. Sol had never expressed needing help beyond his own. She read the insecurity there and, trying to comfort him, laid her hand against his cheek briefly before letting it fall.

"Help from who, Priestess?" he asked. He watched her face as she drew in a deep steadying breath and turned her gaze to meet his.

"My sisters."

To be Continued

Acknowledgements

For my Shelly: thank you for loving me, inspiring me, challenging me and never letting go of my hand. This book would not have happened without you.

To Boss Lady (Debbie McGowan) and others at Beaten Track Publishing: thank you so much for believing in my story and making my dream come true.

Thank you to Carina Campbell-Gedge for designing the perfect and beautiful front cover.

Thank you to everyone who would listen to me getting excited about this story I was writing for 7 years and now you are finally able to read it.

Finally a heart felt thank you to all of my very own Angels without wings. I am privileged and lucky enough to have too many in my life to name, but I know you're there.

Lightning Source UK Ltd.
Milton Keynes UK
UKOW04f0612010714

234326UK00001B/31/P